PUFFIN BOOKS

NAPPER'S GOLDEN GOALS

The beginning of the new football season brings fresh challenges and difficulties to Red Row school's football team. Competing for the first time ever in the Primary Schools League, the Red Row Stars come up against teams of varying ability, some of whom kick on sight. The stars take a lot of knocks and learn some unexpected footballing lessons as the competition progresses.

Can they win the title at the first attempt? It's quite a challenge. The bulk of their new 'star' player, Eddie Boomer, ought to help, but at times he confuses his own side as much as he worries the opposition.

strategies to help them win matches is full of tips and strategies the exciting series follow

Martin Waddell was born and educated in Northern Ireland and his great interests in life are writing and football. Before turning to write he worked in publishing, bookselling and bank-clerking. He has written a great number of books for children and adults. He also writes under the name of Catherine Sefton, and many of these titles He is actively involved with the Arts Council promoting children's writing in schools. He lives in County Down with his wife and three children.

Other books by Martin Waddell

NAPPER GOES FOR GOAL
NAPPER STRIKES AGAIN
TALES FROM THE SHOP THAT NEVER SHUTS

for younger readers

CLASS THREE AND THE BEANSTALK
THE GHOST FAMILY ROBINSON

Picture Book

GOING WEST (with Philippe Dupasquier)

Martin Waddell

Napper's Golden Goals

Illustrated by Barrie Mitchell

Puffin Books

PUFFIN BOOKS

Published by the Penguin Group
Penguin Books Ltd, 27 Wrights Lane, London W8 5TZ, England
Penguin Books USA Inc., 375 Hudson Street, New York, New York 10014, USA
Penguin Books Australia Ltd, Ringwood, Victoria, Australia
Penguin Books Canada Ltd, 10 Alcorn Avenue, Toronto, Ontario, Canada M4V 3B2
Penguin Books (NZ) Ltd, 182–190 Wairau Road, Auckland 10, New Zealand

Penguin Books Ltd, Registered Offices: Harmondsworth, Middlesex, England

First published 1984
10 9 8 7 6 5 4

Printed in England by Clays Ltd, St Ives plc
Set in Monophoto Baskerville

A book for
CENTRAL SWIFTS
(in memory of muddy days!)
and also for co-author Ben Malone,
who wrote one line!

Contents

Top row (L. to R.): J. Deacon   J. Ramsey   S. Rodgers
D. Wilson   D. Forbes   T. Prince   S. Watts
J. Small   H. Haxwell   D. Rooney
Bottom Row (L. to R.): C. Small   M. Bellow   N. McCann
P. Scott   H. Brown   E. Boomer   D. King

1. Championship Challengers!

This is the world-famous Red Row Stars First Team Squad that made school history by competing in the Primary Schools League for the first time ever!

I am Napper McCann, the Demon Goalscorer and Skipper of the team, and that is why I am holding the ball. Terence Prince is our india-rubber goalie; he's the one with the cap and gloves. Cyril Small and Harry Haxwell are our chief defenders and Harpur Brown is our schemer. The one who looks as if he walks through walls is Eddie Boomer, our new signing, and the lot at the back with the Red Row sign are our Official Supporters' Club. Ugly Irma Bankworth is the one with the chewing-gum all over her face.

Mr Hope, our Headmaster, got us new jerseys to play in the Primary Schools League. They are red, with yellow numbers, and a badge like a star for Red Row Stars. The Baboon let us put them on and pose for our picture before our first training session.

'Say cheese!' the Baboon said (the Baboon is Miss Fellows, who helps with the team when Mr Hope can't get to matches) and we did, and this is what happened next.

Cyril fell into the bucket and the water went all over my sister, Avril.

'You did that deliberately, Eddie Boomer!' Avril shouted. 'You stood up so the bench would over-balance!'

'*Boom-Boom!*' said Eddie, and that made Avril even madder.

'Children!' said the Baboon, and she told off Eddie and Harry and Scottie Watts. Then she made us change out of our jerseys for training, so that they would be clean for our first match in the League, which was to be against Monk Noxon Primary School.

'I'll get you later,' Avril said to Eddie.

'You and whose army?' Boom-Boom said. We call Eddie 'Boom-Boom' because that is what he is like. He is always booming into things.

'Me and her!' said Ugly Irma Bankworth, sticking her nose in.

'You look out, Eddie,' said Cyril. 'Irma'll make you a prisoner in her bubble-gum! She'll blow a specially big boomer bubble and you'll never escape!'

Avril went squelching off. It served her right for sticking her ugly self in our team photo. She and Irma had invented the Supporters' Club so that they could persuade Miss Fellows to let them be in the photo.

We hadn't time to waste worrying about them. We had to get on with our training. It was only the second day of term, Thursday, but on Saturday we were due to take the field in our first-ever match in the Primary Schools League. We had decided that we had to have a training session. Mr Hope couldn't make it, so the Baboon was in charge.

'Do whatever Mr Hope usually makes you do,' she said. We split into groups to practise skills. I went with Daniel Rooney and Terence, and this is what we did. Mr Hope calls it 'Shooting Tennis'.

The idea is to have a small goal, about half the usual size, in the middle of the pitch. It's like a tennis net, with a player on each side of it. The two players have to try to beat the goalie. If the goalie saves a shot, he has to spin round and throw it to the player behind him. If the goalie misses the shot, the player behind him gets it anyway. If the ball hits the goalie and he can't hold it, the striker follows up and sticks it past him. Terence says it really tires him out because he has to keep spinning round and facing new situations, but he says that it is brilliant for sharpening his reflexes, and the same goes for us. You have to be on your toes to snatch half-chances in matches. The whole exercise is done very close to goal, so that everyone has to react super-fast.

We did that, and then we did some individual ball work, and some control races where you have two teams and they race against each other, dribbling round markers and finishing off with a pass.

Then we played an eight-a-side across the playground and my team won. I scored twice and saved a penalty. We finished off our training session by practising our set pieces for free kicks and dead-ball situations and our Secret Signs.

'What Secret Signs?' asked Eddie. He'd never heard of Secret Signs. He used to play football at St Joseph's School in Crimpton, and they never had Secret Signs. It was Harpur who thought of having them at our school. They are very good.

We showed him Number Three, the Peel-Off. It is one we use for free kicks on the edge of the area. Harpur is our dead-ball expert, so he gives the Secret Sign. This is Number Three:

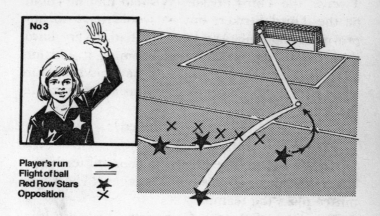

No 3

Player's run →
Flight of ball ⇒
Red Row Stars ★
Opposition ✕

This is what happens:

1. The other team makes a wall to block our free kick, and Cyril and I line up *with* them! We keep backing into their wall, but Cyril does it in the middle of the wall, and I move towards one end. By this time everybody is jostling.

2. Harpur runs up to take the free kick, looking as if he is going to blast it. But he doesn't blast it. He chips it over the wall, and just at that moment I peel off round the side.

Another GREAT Napper McCann SUPER GOAL!

'I'd rather blast it first time,' Eddie said.

We told him our Secret Signs worked, and we showed him the Decoy, which is Number Sixteen, and Number Two, the Shuffle, and Number Twelve, the Third Striker. We told him he could be the Third Striker, but he would have to improve his shooting. We knew he had a very hard shot, but he just went round booming it with no sense of direction. We told him he would have to learn all our Secret Signs if he was going to be in the team.

'Will I be in the team?' he asked.

'Course you will,' said Harry.

'That's up to the Selection Committee,' said Terence Prince, who is our Manager. 'The Committee picks the team.'

'Who is the Selection Committee?' asked Eddie.

'They are,' said Harry. 'Harpur and Cyril and Napper and Terence. So we know four people who are *always* in the team, don't we?'

Harry could have been on the Committee if he had wanted to be, but he didn't want to do anything. We thought of having the team ourselves and went to Mr Hope and he said we could. We arranged everything, and that is why we are the Committee. There was a special meeting of all footballers at Red Row School, and we were elected. Terence is Manager, and Harpur is Hon. Secretary and Cyril is Hon. Treasurer. I was elected

Captain because it was my idea to have a team in the first place.

We got the team started and we called ourselves Red Row Stars. We did very well, but we hadn't won anything so far. We all reckoned the Primary Schools League was our big chance because we would be up against players of our own age. We knew most of the teams and we reckoned we could beat them!

It was up to the Red Row Stars Selection Committee to pick our best team for our first-ever League match, against Monk Noxon Primary School.

This is the team list we put on the school notice-board:

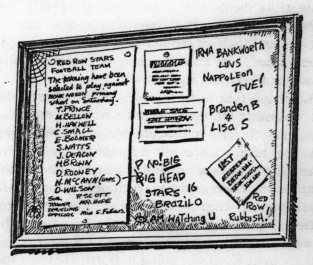

'Boomer?' said Mr Hope when he saw the team sheet.

'He's new, Sir,' I said.

'I know that,' said Mr Hope. 'I'm surprised to see him in the team, that's all. Has anyone seen him play in a match?'

'He's BIG, Sir, big!' said Cyril. 'We need big players, and he's bigger than anybody else in the school.' Cyril was right. Red Row is such a small school that to begin with we thought we wouldn't have enough players to make a decent team. We managed in the end by putting in titchy P4s like Jonathan Ramsey.

'Well, you pick the team,' said Mr Hope. 'We agreed on that when you began. I'm only the trainer. It seems a risk to throw somebody you haven't seen play into an important match, but it is up to you. However, you're going to have to make one change, I'm afraid.' Then he told Cyril that Cyril couldn't play in the match!

Cyril is a first team regular, but he hurt his leg last term. Mr Hope said that he would have to see Cyril play a proper practice match and do some training before we could put him back into the team. Cyril was very cross because the doctor had told his mum he could play, and Mrs Small told Mr Hope. Mr Hope said that that didn't make any difference; he was responsible for boys under his charge, and he couldn't let us risk Cyril.

I thought Cyril was going to burst. He went red,

then he started to argue, and then he went all gulpy. Mr Hope wouldn't listen.

'Tough luck, Cyril,' Terence said when Mr Hope had gone.

'Tough luck on us,' Harpur said. 'We'll lose the match.'

'Oh no, you won't!' said Cyril. And he shouted, 'WE ARE THE CHAMPIONS!' and we all shouted too. We reckoned we could lick Monk Noxon School even without Cyril, and then we would be on our way to winning our first-ever League championship and we'd be champions of Barnleck and prove we really were STARS!

The following teams will take part in this term's competition, playing each other ONCE only, on a round-by-round basis:

> St Gabriel's P.S., Barnleck
> John Abbott P.S., Crown Road, Warne
> Langland P.S., Wythecliffe
> Mill Lane P.S., Mill Lane, Barnleck
> Monk Noxon P.S., Riverdale
> Red Row P.S., Barnleck

FIRST-ROUND MATCHES ARE AS FOLLOWS:
> Mill Lane v. Langland
> Red Row v. Monk Noxon
> St Gabriel's v. John Abbott

Mr P. Sherrard of Mill Lane Primary will act as coordinator of fixtures, which will be played off by arrangement between the two schools concerned. It is IMPORTANT that each round of fixtures should be completed before the next round commences, and those responsible are asked to bear this in mind when making arrangements.

Dr Murray has provided a cup which will be presented to the winners of this year's competition, and medals will be presented to the winners and runners-up. As usual, the Sherrard Cup will be presented to the team with the greatest number of fair-play points at the end of the competition.

D. W. Overend (Secretary)

2. Red Row Stars v. Monk Noxon

PRIMARY SCHOOLS LEAGUE
FIRST ROUND
Red Row P.S. v. Monk Noxon P.S.
Referee: H. Death
Venue: Rec. Field, Barnleck

This is how our team lined up for Red Row Stars' first-ever League championship match:

T. Prince

M. Bellow   H. Haxwell   E. Boomer   S. Watts

J. Deacon   H. Brown

D. Rooney   N. McCann (Capt.)   P. Scott   D. Wilson

Substitute   D. Forbes

Travelling Official   Miss E. Fellows

We thought that it was our best team, almost. The almost was because of Cyril being off the bench. He turned up at school for the game looking really gloomy, and he didn't make any of his Cyril jokes.

We put on our new jerseys. They were brilliant! We had red shirts and red socks to match our jerseys. A lot of parents and little kids from our school

urned up to watch us wearing them and challeng-
ng for the League title. We had a real crowd and a
Big Match atmosphere when I led Red Row Stars
out on to the Rec. field!

The referee, H. Death, blew his whistle, and I
ran up to the centre and shook hands with the
Captain of the other team, Monk Noxon. That was
the team's name, Monk Noxon Primary School,
not the Captain's name. The Captain was Che
Walls. I knew all about him because I had played
five-a-side with him at the Youth Club.

'Who is that fat gook in your team?' Che asked
me.

'Eddie Boomer,' I said. 'He's our new signing.'

'Oh yeah?' said Che. 'You'll need all the big fat
gooks you can get if you're playing us.'

I grinned at him. That was just like Che. We
knew most of the Monk Noxon players, and we
thought we could beat them. Che himself was the
big danger, backed up by Zico Ryan and Squid
Jones in their forward line, with Ron Peirce and
Cormac Thomas in the backs. The rest of them we
didn't know, although Joe Fish of St Gabriel's had
told me the goalie was good. They were bigger
than we were, but not much, and they certainly
hadn't anybody as big as Eddie. We reckoned we
could beat them if we buttoned up Che and Zico
and I slammed in a few Super Goals!

'I'll *wallop* Che Walls!' Cyril said when we heard
who we had to play in the first round, but we had

had to hand the job to Eddie Boomer when Cyril couldn't play. We'd seen enough of Eddie to know he was a tough tackler, and big enough to look after himself if he didn't run out of puff through being so fat. That left Harry Haxwell to pin down Zico, and Harpur to take care of Squid if Scotty couldn't manage him. If Scotty could, we would push Harpur forward to link up with the three front runners, Daniel Rooney, Demon Goalscorer N McCann (Super Star) and Dribbler. P. Scott should have been substitute, but he had had to come in for Cyril, so we had stuck him among the forwards and hoped he might do something. Some hope! Peter is our statue! We told Peter that if he didn't run about a bit, we would pull him off at half-time and put on Duncan Forbes in his place. Duncan isn't bad, but he gets knocked off the ball.

We went into the attack straight from the kick-off, and right away Ron Peirce showed that he was no dozer. First he caught me in a slide-tackle when I broke clear down the right, and then he nipped in to cut off a long ball from Harpur which was aimed for Dribbler, who had got away from the redhead who was marking him. Ron cut the ball out neatly and played it downfield towards Zico Ryan.

Zico is only a little kid, like Dribbler, but he is clever. He got the ball, showed it to Harpur, and then jinked past him. Harry came at him, and Zico sent him one way and went the other. He ran on, committing Scotty to the tackle. Scotty went slithering in and Zico nutmegged him! Zico was clean through, haring for our goal with Boom-Boom tearing across like a mad windmill to cut him off! That left Che Walls unmarked.

Zico got to the edge of our area with Boom-Boom pounding after him, and chipped the ball towards the far post. It was a great ball, drifting across the face of our goal, just beyond Terence's reach. Terence was stranded, and Che Walls came steaming in to head home.

Che never reached the ball.

Marky Bellow went mad! He stuck out a foot and tripped Che! Che went smashing down, and the ref's whistle blasted.

Penalty!

All the Monk Noxon spectators were going mad! A penalty in the first five minutes of the game! The referee went over to Marky and started talking to him. I thought he was giving Marky a warning, but Marky said something and the ref stuck his arm in the air and pointed to the dressing-room.

Marky had been sent off!

'Augh, ref!' Harry shouted.

The ref had Harry over as well.

'Better watch it, or you'll have no players left,' said Che Walls.

The ref didn't send Harry off, and nobody else risked it!

'Deliberate foul, preventing a goal,' said Harpur. 'What did he expect?'

'He'd still be on the field if he'd kept his mouth shut,' said Terence. Then he told us what Marky had called the ref.

Old Marky went off with his head hanging and Che stuck the ball on the penalty spot and got ready to take the kick. He had to wait because Zico was limping around, and their trainer had to come on.

'What happened to him?' I asked.

'I tackled him,' said Boom-Boom. 'I was a bit late, that's all.'

I looked at Harpur. Harpur shrugged. Marky sent off, a penalty kick given away, Harry's name in the book and Boom-Boom crashing into people. It wasn't a good start.

'You want to watch this ref, Eddie,' I said. 'We don't want anybody else sent off.'

'Hardly touched him,' said Eddie, and he walked away.

Che took the spot kick.

It was a great shot, hard and to the left, but Terence somehow got his fingers to it. The ball banged against the post and came out again, but Che, who had kept moving, smacked it back into our net.

1–0 to Monk Noxon.

'You all stood looking at it!' Terence shouted.

He was disgusted. He had made a brilliant save, and nobody had followed up in case there was a rebound!

Mr Hope has coached us to follow up on penalties

at either end of the field, just in case the ball comes back off the keeper or the posts. You have to be sure not to enter the area before the ball is kicked, but otherwise you should follow the ball in as quickly as possible. Terence was right to be mad. We had given away a soft goal.

'Come on, you Stars!' I shouted, and I started clapping my hands and getting at them. We went into the attack, minus Peter Scott. We had had to move him back into defence, into John Deacon's position, because John had gone to right-back to replace Marky. That weakened our midfield, and practically guaranteed that Harpur couldn't come forward. He was stuck with helping Harry against Zico, who was turning out to be more of a handful than we'd reckoned. Peter didn't help Harpur much. All he did was to trot around wondering why nobody was passing to him.

We got clear in the middle, with Ron Peirce short on cover, and two of us against him. I had the ball and I drew Ron and slipped the ball inside to Daniel Rooney. Ron piled into me, and I went down, but Daniel was on his way.

Daniel brought the ball forward into the penalty area and their goalie, Williams, came rushing out of goal and spreadeagled himself like an international. It was a great save. He took the ball clean off Daniel's foot, and Daniel ended up in the Monk Noxon net without the ball.

Williams got up and cleared the ball to Squid,

their right-wing. He was unmarked because Harpur and Harry were busy looking for Zico and Scotty was asleep. He controlled the ball and passed it inside to Che. Che got it, but he hesitated for a moment and it proved fatal. Boom-Boom came tearing up behind him, arms all over the place, and crashed into Che's back.

The whistle went.

Boom-Boom got a talking-to. He stood there listening to it as if it wasn't happening to him. He had his hands on his hips and he was chewing gum.

Free kick!

Not just a free kick, but a dangerous one on the edge of our area.

Zico took the free kick, and drifted it across our goal. Terence didn't come out, and Che got up over Harpur to head the ball. Terence had to turn it over for a corner.

Ron Peirce came trotting up the field and I went after him. Three times already Ron had floored me when I looked as if I might have a chance, so I thought it was time I got my own back. At the same time Daniel spotted me moving back, and he moved infield so that he could break down the centre if we got the ball. Cormac Thomas spotted him and trotted after him. Daniel is always on the look-out for breakaways like that, but Ron and Cormac had things taped.

Ron made a run for the near post as the ball

came over from Zico, who seemed to take all their
dead-ball kicks. It was a decoy run because the ball
was aimed deep for our box. Terence started out of
goal, saw that the ball was drifting away from him,
and hesitated. Eddie and Harpur both went for it,
but Squid Jones got in before them. It was a bad
header, but the ball almost dropped over Terence's
head into the back of our net. Harry Haxwell saved
us when he popped up on the line and headed over
the bar for another corner.

Squid had gone down in a bundle after he headed
the ball. He got up clutching his ribs and said
something to Eddie Boomer.

Boom-Boom just grinned at him.

'Where did you get him, Napper? The Zoo?' said
Che.

The corner came over. Che went for the ball
with Eddie and Harry. He beat them both all ends
up, but his header flashed wide of the post.

'Who was marking him?' Terence shouted.
Boom-Boom should have been, but then Boom-
Boom was busy marking everybody. Wherever the
ball went, he went, and Harry and Harpur were
getting mixed up because of him.

'Sort it out!' Terence shouted.

'What are you sticking to your line for?' Harpur
shouted at Terence. 'That was your ball.'

'I've got no cover,' Terence said.

'Your man, Eddie!' Harry said.

'You got in my way,' Eddie said.

They were all arguing as Terence took the goal kick. Dribbler got the ball and did a little waltz round the guy who was supposed to be marking him. Cormac moved across to cut Dribbler off, and Dribbler heard somebody shouting for it. He thought it was Scotty, and he was surprised because Scotty doesn't overlap much. Anyway, he drew Cormac and then played the ball down towards the corner flag. Old Eddie went steaming after it like a jet-propelled windmill.

Boom-Boom got to the ball and hit a screamer right across the goal. It was meant to be a shot, even though he was at a silly angle to try a shot from, but it turned into a cross. I made a brilliant full-length dive and connected for what I thought was going to be the Napper McCann Super Goal of the Century, but somehow their goalie Williams got down and turned it into the Save of the Century instead! He held on to the ball, one-handed, down by the post. It was incredible. The Monk Noxon fans went mad cheering him.

Here is Williams making his save:

Williams cleared the ball to Squid, who took a wild swing at it and missed, which wrong-footed everybody.

Zico Ryan was first to wake up, and he beat Harry to the ball. For once Zico didn't dribble. He met the ball first time as Harry came in to slide-tackle him, and pushed it into the path of Che Walls. With Harry out of position and Eddie still puffing his way back from the corner flag, Harpur had to commit himself against Che. Harpur almost made it, but as he came across Zico kept on moving the other way. Che let Harpur get across to him, and then simply laid the ball on for Zico.

Zico Ryan collected, carried the ball into our area and boomeranged it over Terence into the back of the net!

2–0 to Monk Noxon.

Here's how Che and Zico did it:

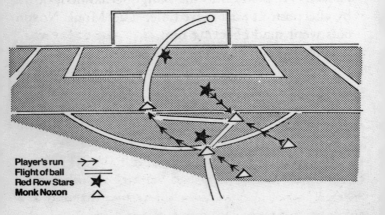

Player's run ⟶⟶
Flight of ball ＝＝
Red Row Stars ★
Monk Noxon △

28

It was a brilliant goal, brilliant because it was so simple. Zico to Che, Che to Zico, BANG . . .! They made it look simple because they seemed to know exactly where to find each other and when to release the ball. Daniel and I had been trying it in practice matches, but we found we couldn't work it in proper games.

'You're going to have to close those two down,' I said to Harry.

'Can't do it on my own!' said Harry.

I told Eddie he had to stick to his position and not go charging off into the attack.

'And if you do, charge back again, twice as fast,' Harpur said.

'Nobody covered for me,' Eddie said.

'Cover back yourself, instead of giving off at other people,' Harpur said to him.

Next time Che got the ball, Eddie really ploughed him from behind, and the whistle went again.

Another free kick.

Zico took it and bent the ball like a banana! It was almost a goal, but somehow Terence managed to get a touch to the ball and send it over for yet another corner.

Off went Zico to take it. He had us guessing every time. Each kick he took was different, and he and Che worked together so well that Che seemed to know exactly what he was going to do. Our big trouble was that nobody had worked out who was marking who, and we were all rushing around at the back giving away oceans of free kicks.

This time, Zico hit the ball across the goal at chest height, aimed for Ron Peirce. Ron thought he was getting it for a near-post flick, but I didn't think so. We both went for the ball, but I got my head to it.

CRACK! Ron's boot took me in the face.

I went down.

The whistle blasted.

'Fifty-fifty ball, ref!' Ron shouted.

I didn't know much about it because I felt as if I had been run over by a bus. Che and Harry and Eddie Boomer carried me off the pitch.

The Baboon came running up. Duncan Forbes was with her. He was stripped off, ready to play.

The Baboon looked at my face. My eye was swollen and there was a cut over it.

'Sorry, Napper,' the Baboon said. 'You'll have to stay off.'

I didn't argue. I was groggy and couldn't see properly. The Baboon brought her car across the grass and the Monk Noxon trainer lifted me into it, all wrapped up in one of the Baboon's blankets. We went off just as the whistle went for the end of the first half.

We were 2–0 down.

The Baboon took me to the doctor, and the doctor got my dad to come. I went to hospital and had some stitches and an X-ray, and then I had to go home and go to bed.

Avril put her head round the door. 'Ya-ha! Stupid little football team lost!' she said. Then she came in and looked at me. 'You look awful,' she said. 'I mean, awfuller than usual.'

'Um,' I said. I couldn't say much else because my mouth was swollen, and the whole side of my face was bruised. I had a plaster over my eye, like a pirate, but I didn't feel like one.

'It was 5–0,' Avril said.

'Umm!'

'You got beat!'

'Ummm!'

'Tell you what,' said Avril. 'If you like, I'll play in your place next week. Bet I'd be better than you.' She went off downstairs shouting about it.

Then she came back upstairs again and said, 'If anybody brings you grapes, bags I some!'

I was fed up. We'd lost the match 5–0, and the way we had been playing it didn't look as if we would ever win anything, let alone the League championship.

I told Cyril they'd have to have an emergency meeting to sort things out, and he said that they would, but it wouldn't do much good because everybody was arguing after the game, and there would be more arguing if they had a meeting. He brought me some grapes and a comic and told me what a rotten match it was to watch.

'They all ran around at the back, tackling nothing and marking each other,' Cyril said. 'Reckon I can sort things out when I make my come-back.'

Then Cyril went off and I went to sleep.

When I woke up again, *somebody* had pinched all my grapes.

PRIMARY SCHOOLS LEAGUE

BULLETIN NO. 2

FIRST-ROUND RESULTS:
Mill Lane 6   Langland 0
Red Row 0   Monk Noxon 5
St Gabriel's 3   John Abbott 3

MILL LANE V. LANGLAND

Last year's League champions, Mill Lane, fielding an experimental line-up, did well to give a convincing account of themselves against a Langland side which still shows room for improvement. Scorers: Beattie (2), Hopper (2), McGaw (2).

RED ROW V. MONK NOXON

As expected, newcomers Red Row were no match for an experienced Monk Noxon team, who ran out the winners of a bad-tempered match. Goalie Prince was best for Red Row, particularly when under heavy pressure in the second half. Ryan, Ambawi and Walls (3) were the scorers for Monk Noxon.

ST GABRIEL'S V. JOHN ABBOTT

This hard-fought encounter was a bruising start to the campaign for both sides! Fish made an outstanding contribution at centre-half for St Gabriel's, helped by strong play by his two full-backs. John Abbott were perhaps fortunate to be on level terms (1–1) at half-time, but rallied well after falling behind early in the second half. Gowland notched a hat-trick for John Abbott, and Bridges, Collins and Cleland replied for St Gabriel's.

LEAGUE TABLE

	P	W	D	L	F	A	Pts
Mill Lane	1	1	0	0	6	0	2
Monk Noxon	1	1	0	0	5	0	2
St Gabriel's	1	0	1	0	3	3	1
John Abbott	1	0	1	0	3	3	1
Red Row	1	0	0	1	0	5	0
Langland	1	0	0	1	0	6	0

SECOND-ROUND FIXTURES:
Langland v. Red Row
St Gabriel's v. Monk Noxon
John Abbott v. Mill Lane

The tie of the round should be the clash between Monk Noxon, who convincingly defeated newcomers Red Row in their opening engagement, and St Gabriel's, who many are already tipping for the title. Langland will be hoping to open their account against a disappointing Red Row, and last year's champions, Mill Lane, will view the visit to Warne to meet John Abbott with some apprehension.

The Committee is concerned about a number of incidents in the first-round games which fell beneath the standard of sportsmanship normally expected in this competition. Referees have been asked to crack down on offenders.

PLEASE NOTE that it is the responsibility of the HOME team to provide proper facilities for the referee. BOTH teams are requested to furnish match details and results to me for inclusion in this bulletin.

D. W. Overend (Secretary)

3. Red Row Stars v. Langland

PRIMARY SCHOOLS LEAGUE
SECOND ROUND
Langland P.S. v. Red Row P.S.
Referee: D. W. Overend
Venue: Wythecliffe Playing Fields

This was the Red Row Stars team that was selected to face Langland in our second League match, a game we couldn't afford to lose if we were to have any hope of winning the title:

T. Prince

M. Bellow   H. Haxwell   C. Small   S. Watts

J. Small   J. Deacon   H. Brown (Capt.)

D. Rooney   E. Boomer   D. Wilson

Substitute   P. Scott

Travelling Official   Miss E. Fellows

It was the first-ever Red Row Stars match without Demon Goalscorer N. McCann! My dad drove me over to Wythecliffe in the van and I was able to watch through the fence. The doctor said I had concussion and I had to stay off school. I wouldn't have minded being at school if I could have played in the team.

That was the team the Selection Committee picked. Terence and Harpur and Cyril picked it. I am the other member of the Selection Committee, but I wasn't there, so I couldn't pick anybody.

They put Eddie Boomer in at striker to replace me, and brought Cyril back in defence to replace Eddie. They dropped Peter Scott to substitute and put Joe Small on in his place. Duncan Forbes couldn't play because he had piano lessons.

'We're going to play 4–3–3 instead of 4–2–4,' Terence said when he came to make sure I couldn't play. 'The Selection Committee decided that there had to be changes.'

'Why?'

'Because we got beaten,' said Terence. 'The Monk Noxon kids went around blowing that we were no good. You should have heard Knocker Lewis and some of his lot from St Gabriel's. They say they're going to pulverize us this term. So we can't go on being beaten, can we? That's why we are changing the way we play.'

I didn't think we had lost against Monk Noxon because of the way we played 4–2–4. I didn't think we had played 4–2–4! It was more like 1–0–0, with Terence doing all the playing and everybody else arguing.

'Wait and see how the new system works,' said Terence.

The first shock I had was when the team came out, because Marky Bellow wasn't there. Then I saw Marky standing on the touchline, and my dad shouted to him and he came over and got in the van with us.

'Why aren't you in the team, Marky?' my dad asked. 'I thought you were a first team regular these days?'

'One-match suspension for being sent off,' Marky said. 'The ref turned out to be the League Secretary, and he told Miss Fellows she hadn't read the rules, and he wouldn't let me play.'

'What did you get sent off for?' my dad asked.

'Nothing,' said Marky, sounding fed up.

They made Scuddy Rodgers sub.

In a way it wasn't a bad thing, because Scuddy was all right at football until he got substituted last term and then for a long time he wouldn't play. He had to be sub, because with Duncan Forbes doing his piano and Jonathan Ramsey off with a cold there wasn't anybody else. Scuddy had come over in Mr Deacon's car to watch the game, and Miss Fellows saw him standing there and said he had to be sub. Scuddy looked quite pleased. I think he was glad to be back in football. John Deacon moved back to take Marky's place, and Peter Scott came into midfield.

This was the final line-up, the team that actually took the field for our first away match in the League:

T. Prince

J. Deacon   H. Haxwell   C. Small   S. Watts

J. Small   P. Scott   H. Brown

D. Rooney   E. Boomer   D. Wilson

Substitute   D. Rodgers

It meant that we were fielding a weakened team, minus N. McCann Super Star and M. Bellow, one of our big players, for what we reckoned would be the most important fixture we would play in the League. If we didn't beat Langland, we would be firmly anchored at the bottom of the table, and St Gabriel's and the other schools would all say we were no use.

We needn't have worried.

We almost scored straight from the kick-off when Dribbler broke away on a long run down the left, beat two men and squared the ball inside to Eddie Boomer. Eddie shot into the side net. He put his head in his hands and made a song and dance about it. But the next time he got the ball, he didn't miss. It was a brilliant high ball from Harpur into the penalty area and Eddie got up above everybody else and slammed home a header into the top corner.

'Don't wreck the van!' my dad said, and Marky and I had to stop thumping each other.

It was Red Row Stars' first-ever League goal scored by stand-in striker E. Boomer with a great rocket header that left the titchy Langland goalie helpless.

Then Dribbler got into business again on the wing. Dribbler is used to being given a hard time by players who are bigger than he is, but the little kid who was marking him hadn't a clue. Dribbler jinked outside him, carried the ball to the line and slung over a high centre. Daniel ran on to it beyond the far post and volleyed it back across the goal. Eddie came running in and met the ball first time with a rocket shot which went straight into the goalie and nearly killed him!

The titchy goalie went down on the line, holding the ball and making noises as if he couldn't breathe. The ref blew his whistle and came running up and the Langland teacher came on to the field and together they got the goalie up. He was all red in the face, and crying. He had to be helped off the field. Another of the Langland players went into goal.

The referee gave a bounce ball about a metre from the goal-line.

Eddie Boomer lined up with one of their defenders.

The ref bounced the ball and Eddie boomed it straight into the back of the net!

2–0 to Red Row Stars! Langland hadn't lined up on their goal-line to stop it.

They were real no-hopers! They hadn't even got a substitute to put on when their goalie went off.

Red Row Stars went on all-out attack!

Cyril came up and had a shot that the goalie – the new goalie – saved, and then Daniel shot wide when Harpur had put him clear in the area. Harry had a shot turned behind for a corner, and Eddie Boomer missed a sitter right in front of the near post. Then Daniel broke down the centre and passed to Eddie, who was in the clear. Eddie hit the ball over the crossbar with the goalie beaten. Eddie put his head in his hands. He couldn't believe it! Harry Haxwell had a shot from outside the area which was a real crasher, and the sub goalie dived and made a super save. The goalie got up, looking for somebody to clear to, and Eddie Boomer came in and bashed right into him.

The ref's whistle went!

D. W. Overend got hold of Eddie and read him a big lecture.

'He's not having any nonsense, that ref, is he?' said my dad.

'You should have seen the one we had last week,' I said. 'He was certain DEATH.' If it had been H. Death, Eddie would have been ordered off.

Harpur spotted a space and made a run from the back and somebody tripped him. That gave us a free kick. I didn't see Harpur make his signal, but I saw Harry Haxwell coming up from the back, and I guessed what that meant. Secret Sign Number Thirteen: Harpur to Daniel, square on the edge of the box, Daniel drifts the ball across the face of the goal, and Super Star N. McCann heads in on the far post. Only H. Haxwell was going to do it instead.

They played it perfectly.

Harry met the ball on the far post and zonked it past the goalie, low down into the corner of the Langland net. Harry got the ball just right on his forehead, heading it down the way Mr Hope showed us.

Harry Haxwell ran up the field cheering and shouting and saying what a great goal it was until the ref called him over and told him to to shut up. Then the ref gave offside against Eddie Boomer, so it was no goal after all.

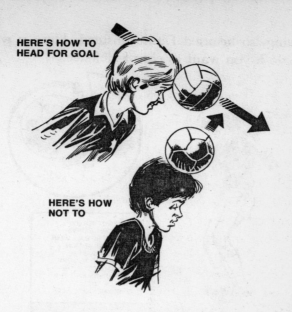

HERE'S HOW TO HEAD FOR GOAL

HERE'S HOW NOT TO

The free kick got the ball into our half, but it came straight back again. Harpur spotted Daniel going on a run down the flank. Harpur chipped the ball over the titchy defenders to land in Daniel's path and Daniel squared the ball first time to Eddie. Eddie took a big swing at it and almost bust the corner flag.

It was a pity that he missed, because it spoiled a brilliant move. Mr Hope had spent ages with Harpur coaching him on how to chip the ball over the defence for someone running on to it. It is a great way to beat a massed defence if you have players who are quick off the mark, like D. Rooney and N. McCann Super Star. N. McCann wasn't playing, so he used Daniel instead. Here is what you do if you want to chip a defence.

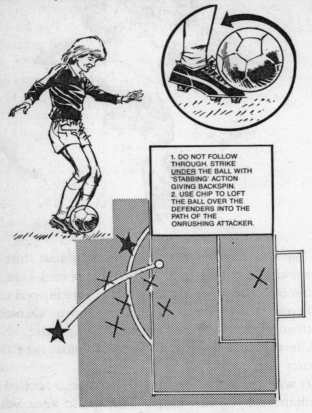

1. DO NOT FOLLOW THROUGH. STRIKE <u>UNDER</u> THE BALL WITH 'STABBING' ACTION GIVING BACKSPIN.
2. USE CHIP TO LOFT THE BALL OVER THE DEFENDERS INTO THE PATH OF THE ONRUSHING ATTACKER.

Mr Hope concentrated on teaching Harpur how to chip, because he says Harpur is the only player we've got who is able to spot openings quickly enough. He says it is up to me and Daniel to make the runs, and up to Harpur to spot us making them.

'Wish I was playing,' I said to Marky.

'I wish you were too,' said Marky. 'We would have had a bagful by now if you were on.'

Harpur decided he wanted to have a go himself, so the next time he came forward he had a shot, but this time the goalie punched clear. The ball came to Dribbler, who lobbed it back cleverly over the goalie's head. It landed on top of the net, but it wouldn't have been a goal anyway because Eddie had run offside. Harpur started moaning to him about it.

'You part with the ball quicker, then I won't get caught,' Eddie said.

The cry-baby goalie came on again. The ref said it was all right for him to come on as they hadn't used a substitute, and he went back into goal.

The first shot he got was another Eddie Boomer special. He saved it well, but Eddie followed up and kicked it out of his arms as the goalie lay on the ground. D. W. Overend gave a foul for dangerous play.

Then Harpur said something to Eddie and Eddie went bonkers. He yelled at Harpur! Harry came running up and got between them, and even Terence started coming out of his goal. We couldn't tell what it was all about because we were too far away in the van.

The Baboon came out from under her tree and shouted at them. She looked crosser than Eddie was.

The next goal came when Boom-Boom got the ball in our half, beat four men and walloped it home from the edge of the area, putting us 3–0 up.

Eddie had got a hat-trick!

Their goalie looked really disgusted with his defenders. They were all small, apart from the centre-half, and he was a kipper! Nobody tried to stop Eddie once he had put his head down and charged at them.

Half-time.

Marky went off to join the team talk, and my dad gave me a half-time orange from the box under his seat. My dad said I had to stay in the van because it was a cold morning and I didn't look well.

'No need for all that fuss about getting you fit for the match, was there, Napper?' my dad said. 'Your new striker is doing a great job.' My dad doesn't know much about football.

'He's called Eddie Boomer,' I said. 'We call him Boom-Boom because he goes around banging into things.'

The referee, D. W. Overend, went over to both teams and talked to them in the interval, and then he had a word with Miss Fellows. The next thing was that we started the second half without Daniel Rooney. Scuddy Rodgers came on in his place.

'What are they doing that for?' I asked, because Scuddy is a pudding!

'I expect your teacher wants to give the other team a chance,' my dad said.

I wasn't happy about that. I wanted Red Row Stars to score bags of goals! It wasn't fair taking Daniel off, because he is one of the deadliest marksmen we have, not counting N. McCann Super Star!

Red Row went straight on to the attack. Harry Haxwell got the ball and went on a run. He fired the ball hard across the goal and wide of the post. I don't know whether it was meant to be a shot or a cross, but anyway it was a bad ball because Eddie was free in front of goal and would probably have scored. The good thing about Eddie's play was the way he kept moving around, so that defenders never knew where he would pop up next. The bad thing was that he kept popping up in offside positions. I bet old D. W. Overend got tired of blowing the whistle at him.

Everybody wanted to score goals. Cyril made a run from the back and tried a long shot, but it was a typical Cyril effort and went miles over the bar.

'Where's your friend?' my dad asked, because Marky hadn't come back to the van.

I didn't know where Marky had gone to, and I hadn't time to worry about it because we got a free kick on the edge of the area. I knew Harpur would take it and use one of our Secret Signs.

This is what Harpur did:

45

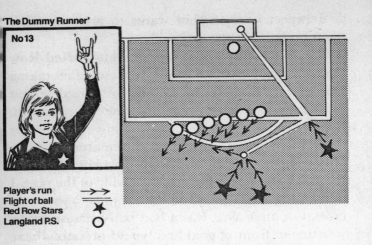

'The Dummy Runner'

No 13

Player's run
Flight of ball
Red Row Stars
Langland P.S.

That is the way it was supposed to work.

Eddie was doing my bit, so he was supposed to be the first man to the ball. His job was to run over it and make the dummy run, drawing the defence while Harry, following up behind him, played the ball sideways for Harpur to hit.

Boom-Boom ran at the ball . . . and BOOMED it! The ball whistled past the wall and past the goal, for a goal kick.

Marky and Daniel came across to the van, and got in beside me in the front seat. There wasn't much room.

'So much for Eddie learning all our Secret Signs if he got in the team!' Daniel said.

The ball came out from the goal kick to the feet of one of their midfield men. He played the ball down the centre and Cyril came across to cut it off, but something went wrong.

The Langland centre-forward was going for it. Usually Cyril would have come in with one of his famous slide-tackles and played the ball safely into touch off the centre-forward, giving us a throw-in. This time he looked as if he was going to do it, then he half hesitated, went in . . . and missed. The centre-forward prodded the ball past him and their right-winger came tearing in and toe-punted it past Terence.

'No cover again!' Terence shouted disgustedly.

'You were picking daisies!' Harry shouted back. Harry had stayed up in the Langland half after the wasted free kick.

Cyril lay on his back, flat out. The goal was his fault, but it wouldn't have happened if anyone else had been back to cover for his mistake.

'That mucks up our goal difference,' Marky said.

Mr Hope had told us that the League would be decided on goal difference if two teams were equal. Goal difference is when you subtract the goals against you from the goals you have scored. We had lost our first match 0–5, and the soft goal we had given away meant that the score against Langland was 3–1, so our goal difference was $3 - 6 = -3$. We weren't going to win anything with a goal difference of -3. Sometimes competitions use goal average, which is the goals for *divided* by the goals against. If the Primary Schools League had been worked on goal average, our average would have been 3 ÷ 6, which equals 0·5. It sounds better than − 3, but it's still rotten!

'Looks like the opposition is going to make a fight of it,' my dad said when he saw that Langland had scored.

Harpur was clapping his hands and shouting at everybody. The Selection Committee had made Harpur Captain because I couldn't play. He was supposed to be in charge of what happened on the field.

The goal wakened Red Row up. First Harry had another go and banged a post, and then Eddie boomed his way down the middle, dumping their centre-half on the seat of his pants and cracking in a shot that missed by a mile. Their little goalie looked as if he was going to run away when he saw Eddie coming.

He got a corner. Harpur took it, and Eddie went up with the keeper. The keeper was so busy looking at Eddie that he muffed his catch and Cyril came sliding in on the goal-line to ram the ball home.

Cyril went mad! It was his come-back game after a long lay-off through injury, and he had scored a vital goal just when it looked as if Langland might get back into the game.

4–1 to Red Row!

Straight away, Eddie got another one. He chased a long ball from Harry into the penalty area. It should have been the cry-baby goalie's ball, but he stayed rooted on his line. Eddie knocked it in for his fourth goal, and ran all the way back to the half-way line with the ball in his arms.

5–1 to Red Row!

After that it was a procession! Everybody came pounding up to try to score, even Scuddy, but in the end Dribbler got one, and Eddie got his fifth goal, and that was all.

Final score: 7–1 to Red Row Stars!

7–1!

The biggest-ever victory in the history of our football team, and I had missed it.

'We are the champions!' Cyril and John Deacon were shouting, and Scottie and Harry and Peter Scott chaired Eddie off the pitch.

Terence walked off on his own, looking fed up. He'd had nothing to do all day except pick one Langland toe-punt out of the back of the net.

'Not much of a match,' said Marky.

'We won, didn't we?' said Daniel.

I didn't say anything. It hadn't really been a football match at all. Our team had run round knocking the little Langland kids over and banging shots at their goalie. Nobody had tried to play football.

Marky and Daniel said they'd see me at school on Monday, and got out of the van. They went over to join the others.

'Okay, Napper?' said my dad. 'Do you want to

drive round by the gates so that you can speak to your friends?'

'No,' I said.

'How does your head feel?'

'All right,' I said. It had to be all right. If it wasn't all right, my dad wouldn't send me to school, and if I wasn't in school on Monday, Mr Hope wouldn't let me play in the team in our next match.

Miss Fellows saw us. She came over to the van and asked my dad how I was. He said I was all right.

'Well, Napper,' she said. 'What did you think of the match?'

'GREAT, Miss,' I said. '7–1!' I didn t really think it was great, but I knew if I said it was a bad match Miss Fellows would think it was only because I wasn't playing.

'Don't get too excited about it,' she said 'The other school had a lot of boys off with flu '

'That explains it!' said my dad.

'Explains what?' I said.

'Well, I've never seen such a small football team, have you?' said my dad.

When we got home, Avril was in the garden with Irma Bankworth. 'Get beaten again?' she shouted.

'7–1!' I shouted. 'We WON!'

'Only because *you* weren't playing,' said Avril.

I went into the house. My mum had the garden sprinkler attached to the hose, which ran to our

yard tap. On my way in the back door, I turned
the tap on.

PRIMARY SCHOOLS LEAGUE

BULLETIN NO. 3

SECOND-ROUND RESULTS:
Langland i   Red Row 7
St Gabriel's 3   Monk Noxon 3
John Abbott 4   Mill Lane 2

LANGLAND V. RED ROW
An under-strength Langland team were convincingly beaten by Red Row in this one-sided match, which featured a brilliant performance by Boomer, who notched five goals. Soley scored for Langland. Wilson and C. Small also scored for the winners.

ST GABRIEL'S V. MONK NOXON
Monk Noxon opened impressively in this game, with Ryan proving a danger in everything he did. However, in the second half St Gabriel's made adjustments to their defensive line-up and took command. Fish had an outstanding game for St Gabriel's, and Monk Noxon have goalkeeper Williams to thank for saving them a point by his second-half display.

JOHN ABBOTT V. MILL LANE
Champions Mill Lane were unsettled by the hard-tackling John Abbott team, for whom Jenson and Gowland were outstanding. Gowland (3) and Priest scored for John Abbott, and Beattie and McGaw replied for Mill Lane, both goals resulting from fine play by Margolis.

LEAGUE TABLE

	P	W	D	L	F	A	Pts
Monk Noxon	1	1	1	0	8	3	3
John Abbott	2	1	1	0	7	5	3
Mill Lane	2	1	0	1	8	4	2
Red Row	2	1	0	1	7	6	2
St Gabriel's	2	0	2	0	6	6	2
Langland	2	0	0	2	1	13	0

THIRD-ROUND FIXTURES:
Red Row v. Mill Lane
St Gabriel's v. Langland
Monk Noxon v. John Abbott

The meeting of the two table-toppers when John Abbott travel to Monk Noxon appears to be the pairing of the round. Meanwhile, champions Mill Lane will no doubt expect to make up lost ground at the expense of new-comers Red Row. Langland will find it hard to take a point from a St Gabriel's side which remains unbeaten after tackling their two main rivals in successive weeks.

D. W. Overend (Secretary)

4. Trouble!

Mr Hope was supposed to take us for training on Wednesday after school, but he had to go to the League meeting and he didn't get back until we were nearly finished. He told us to play an eight-a-side, ten minutes each way, and when that was finished he told us to get changed and come to the P7 Room because he wanted to talk to us.

'What's all this about?' Cyril asked when we were changing.

Nobody knew.

We got changed and went to the P7 Room.

Mr Hope came in.

'Everybody here?' he said, and he counted us. Everybody was there except John Deacon, who had had to go home early because he did a paper round.

'Right!' said Mr Hope. 'I'm sorry I couldn't get to your last two games, but I've been busy on other matters. However, I've heard quite a bit from other sources about what has been happening.'

'7–1, Sir!' said Cyril.

'I don't think that Langland School are exactly

Brazil, Cyril,' said Mr Hope. 'Won one, lost one, so your results aren't bad.'

'I'm sorry we lost the first match, Sir,' said Harpur. 'We were dead unlucky. Marky got sent off and Napper got hurt and –'

'Sorry?' said Mr Hope, raising his eyebrows. 'Sorry, sorry, sorry?' Mr Hope often says things three times like that. 'I'm *not* sorry you lost to Monk Noxon School, Harpur.'

Harpur didn't say anything more. We had a good idea what was coming next. Mr Hope was cross about what Marky had said to the referee.

'You had a hard time of it last season in the Youth League. You were up against players who were much bigger than yourselves, and one or two of the less skilful sides gave you a battering you didn't deserve. But you played good football and you did well, all things considered. From what I hear of the Monk Noxon game, you were up against a team of boys the same age as yourselves, a team with at least one player of exceptional ability.'

'Monk Noxon weren't all that cop, Sir,' said Harry. 'We were sloppy at the back.'

'Only Zico Ryan was good, Sir,' said Terence.

'Zico's brilliant!' I said.

'It is not the Monk Noxon performance that concerns me,' said Mr Hope. 'It is the way *you* played. I've spoken to Mr Death and Mr Overend. Mr Death tells me that in his opinion the Monk Noxon match was spoiled by the behaviour of *one* of the teams, and in Mr Overend's view the match against Langland wasn't much better.'

'Only we won it!' said Cyril. '7–1!'

'I'm not concerned with the score,' said Mr Hope. 'It's the way you've been playing that worries me.'

'We were only trying to win, Sir,' said Cyril.

'We've got to try to win, Sir,' said Harry. 'That's what it's all about, isn't it?'

'Is it?' said Mr Hope.

Nobody said anything. We all thought it *was*. We thought it would be no good having a football team if everybody beat us.

'What about a team like Langland?' said Mr Hope. 'What should they do? Give up and go home because you beat them?'

'Might as well,' said Cyril.

'I seem to remember losing a match 8–1 not so long ago,' said Mr Hope.

'That was before we got properly organized, Sir,' I said. 'We're much better now.'

'Yes,' said Mr Hope. 'You are. You've begun to play as a team, or I thought you had. But now I gather that you have picked up something else as well as teamwork. You've been dishing it out on the field! Laying into the other teams, and fighting amongst yourselves. Giving cheek to referees!'

We all looked at Marky.

'I didn't do anything to get sent off *for*,' Marky mumbled.

'I'll see you about that matter later, Bellow,' said Mr Hope.

'The ref liked the sound of his whistle, Sir,' said Harry.

'The free kicks were all one way, according to Miss Fellows,' said Mr Hope.

We knew why that was. That was Boom-Boom booming, but we couldn't say that to Mr Hope. That was one of the reasons why Terence and Cyril and Harpur had decided to move him out of defence for the second game.

'You are supposed to be learning how to *play* football!' said Mr Hope. 'Some of you could . . . *will* . . . be good footballers one day . . . if, *if* you keep at it. *If* you think about your game, *if* you keep training, *if* you work on your skills, *if* you can remember *always* to play as a team, and not as individuals. Going out and trying to walk all over the opposition is no way to play football.'

'The others have more players to chose from than we have, Sir,' said Terence. 'We've got to show them we are as good as they are. That means our big ones have got to go in hard, because they have to cover for the small ones.' We were glad Terence said it, because he was the one player who couldn't be got at for dirty play. He was the goalie, and he didn't get involved in tackles.

'I want you to go in *hard* . . . hard and *fair*! That's one thing. Throwing your weight about on a football pitch is quite another. I'd rather you were beaten every week, like Langland . I'd rather you had no team at all, if that is what you are going to do. If you want to have a football team at Red Row School, then you can have one. A team where you learn something about the game. That's fine! But if you want a team that wins because people are afraid to play against you, forget it! I am *not*, *not*, repeat N O T, going to have the name of this school linked with the sort of behaviour which has been reported to me. That means your behaviour towards the opposition, the referee and *each other*!'

He stopped.

'Well?' he said.

Nobody felt like saying anything. He didn't know what it had been like. Old Death the referee was stupid. We didn't think our game with Monk Noxon had been bad, and it wasn't our fault that Langland had a titchy team and a cry-baby goalie.

'Are you going to play football or kick people?' Mr Hope said.

'Play football, Sir,' Terence and I said.

'Well, I hope so,' said Mr Hope. 'Hope, Hope, Hope! That's my name, and that's my nature! I *hope* you do well on Saturday morning against Mill Lane. I'm going to be there and I'll have something to say to you all if matters don't improve.'

Then he told us we could go.

'I don't know what all the fuss is about,' said Harpur as we walked across the playground. 'We weren't rough. And he told us to keep talking on

58

the field, telling each other what was going wrong.'

'It's only Miss Fellows,' Scotty said. 'The Baboon doesn't know what playing football is like.'

'What about Eddie?' said Harpur when we were coming out of the gates.

'What about Eddie?'

'Eddie's rough,' said Harpur.

'He's not rough,' said Cyril. 'He's just big. He knocks people over without meaning to.'

'Like the Langland goalie,' said Terence.

'That's the way Eddie plays,' said Cyril. 'That's why he's a brilliant striker.'

'He's not brilliant,' said Harpur.

'Eddie scores goals,' said Cyril.

'Napper is our best goalscorer,' Terence said.

'Napper never got five goals in one game, did you, Napper?' said Cyril.

'Doesn't matter!' said Terence. 'Napper's still the KING!'

'I reckon we should drop Boom-Boom,' said Harpur. 'He may be big, but he doesn't pass the ball. He just runs around muddling everybody up.'

'We can't drop him after five goals,' said Terence.

'We need big players,' I said.

'If Boom-Boom goes on knocking people over, Mr Hope might get really mad and withdraw us from the League,' said Harpur.

'He couldn't,' said Cyril, but we all knew that he could.

Terence was the elected Manager of the team, so we reckoned it was up to him. He said, 'I think the

Selection Committee should have a deputation and speak to Eddie. The deputation will have to tell him that he's to stop kicking people or he's out. How's that?'

'The Captain should do it,' said Harpur.

'Which Captain?' said Cyril. 'You or Napper?'

'Both,' said Harpur.

I was glad he said it, because I reckoned it would look bad if I started telling Boom-Boom off when he had taken my place and scored five goals in one match.

'I'll come because I'm Manager and I ought to,' said Terence.

We told Boom-Boom the next day at break.

'You're all soft at this school,' he said, but he said he would try not to bash into people. 'It's just the way I play,' he said. 'Boom-Boom!'

'I don't think he took us seriously,' I said to Terence afterwards. Terence said we would just have to wait and see how it worked out on the pitch.

We had enough to worry about without having to think about Mr Hope withdrawing us from the League. We were down to tackle the League champions, Mill Lane. They were level on points with us in the League after two games, but above us on goal difference. The bulletin said they ought to beat us, so we reckoned we were in for a very tough match which we had to win if we were to keep in touch with the leaders!

5. Red Row Stars v. Mill Lane

PRIMARY SCHOOLS LEAGUE
THIRD ROUND
Red Row P.S. v. Mill Lane P.S.
Referee: Mr Deacon
Venue: Rec. Field, Barnleck

Our third match in the League turned out to be the most difficult game we had ever faced, because we had to play against the defending League champions without FIVE of our best players.

On Thursday Harry Haxwell, Dribbler Wilson and Scotty Watts didn't turn up at school, and on Friday Mrs Brown rang Mr Hope and told him that Harpur had flu, and on Saturday Helena Bellow came down to school on her bicycle and told Mr Hope that old Marky had a temperature. His mum said he had to stay in bed, even though Marky didn't want to.

We had NO team, almost!

'Sir, Sir! We'll have to call off the match, Sir!' said Cyril.

'Why?'

'Sir, Sir, because we haven't got enough players, Sir,' said Cyril.

'Yes, we have,' said Mr Hope. We counted and we only had ten players, so Mr Hope sent Cyril on his bicycle to fetch Douglas King from the fourth year and tell him to bring his boots because he was playing in the team.

I was thinking.

'Sir?' I said. 'What about Helena, Sir?'

The thing is, we all know Helena can play. She is probably better than old Marky.

'Well, Helena?' said Mr Hope.

Helena went bright red.

'There is absolutely N O reason why you shouldn't play in the team, Helena, if you want to,' said Miss Fellows.

'Quite right!' said Mr Hope, and then he added; 'But only if you want to.'

'You go home on your bike and borrow Marky's boots,' I said.

'Marky has gi-normous feet!' said Terence.

'Well, we could get Dribbler's then,' said John Deacon.

'Helena?' said Miss Fellows.

Helena shook her head.

'Sure?' said Miss Fellows.

'Yes, Miss,' said Helena. I was really mad at her and I got her later and made her tell me why. She said it was because of Avril and Ugly Irma Bank-worth; they called her names for playing football and that was why she didn't want to be in the team. She said that Avril and Irma had started an Anti-Football-Team Club. I told her I would get Avril for her, but it didn't do any good.

'I don't want crummy girls in the team, anyway,' said Cyril, when he came back and heard about it. 'Girls can't play football.'

'Don't let Miss Fellows hear you, that's all!' said Terence. Miss Fellows says girls can do anything boys can, only better!

'You can be Knickers United, I'm not,' said Cyril. The trouble was that we knew that Knocker Lewis and the Clelands and most of the St Gabriel's team would be on the touchline, because Knocker had told us they were coming to see us get hammered by the League champions. We could imagine what they would call us if we had girls in our team.

'You're all right,' said Mr Hope. 'You've got eleven players.'

'No sub, Sir,' said Cyril.

'Then you'll have to manage without one, won't you, Cyril?' said Mr Hope. 'Pick a team with a sound defence, and try to score on breakaways. Build from the back. Defend for the first five minutes. Then, if they turn out to be not as good as you think they are, you can switch people round and start attacking.'

'Some hope, Sir,' said Cyril glumly. We thought Cyril was right. Half our team had flu, and the match should have been called off because if we lost with half a team, we would have only two points out of three matches, and absolutely no chance of winning the League.

'Perhaps you won't lose,' said Mr Hope. 'Who knows? There are only eleven of them.'

'They're the defending champions, Sir,' said Cyril. 'It isn't fair.'

'Do your best,' said Mr Hope. 'But remember . . . NO ROUGH STUFF!'

This is the team we picked from what was left of the Red Row Stars:

T. Prince
S. Rodgers   J. Deacon   C. Small   J. Small
D. Rooney   P. Scott   N. McCann (Capt.)
J. Ramsey   E. Boomer   D. King
Substitute   N. O. Body!
Trainer   Mr Hope
Travelling Official   Miss E. Fellows

The idea was that John Deacon and Cyril would play deep, trying to cover Scuddy Rodgers and Joe Small, with Daniel and me in front of them, so that we would have hard tacklers at the heart of our defence. Daniel and I would go forward if we got the chance, and we would try to lay on chances for Eddie Boomer. We told Boom-Boom to chase everything and try to thump in some goals, and Jonathan Ramsey and little Douglas King were to help him.

'Do your best, Son,' Mr Hope said to little Douglas. 'Nobody is going to shout at you if you do something wrong.'

Douglas was very excited. I had to help him to tie up his boots. Jonathan Ramsey had to play in plimsolls because he'd left his boots at home.

'Here come Nappy United!' Knocker Lewis shouted when he saw all the little ones. Then he went on and on about how we'd have to change their nappies at half-time.

Joe Fish and Neil Collins and the Clelands and Knocker had all come over to see our match. They were lined up on the touchline. Their match wasn't till the afternoon. We weren't surprised to see them. The Stringy Pants are our biggest rivals. We call them the Stringy Pants because they used to have shorts held up with string, and their shorts fell down.

'You'll laugh on the other side of your face when we play you, Knocker!' Cyril told him, and Joe Fish told Knocker to shut up. Knocker didn't. He went behind our goal and kept on shouting at Terence. Terence didn't take any notice, or not much anyway.

'Who is that creep doing all the shouting?' Eddie Boomer asked me.

'Knocker Lewis. He's in the Stringy Pants team, St Gabriel's. He thinks he's tough.'

'Does he?' said Eddie. 'We'll see about that.'

I was Captain again because I was fit and back in the team. I would have been centre-forward, but we couldn't risk putting Eddie in defence in case he gave away lots of free kicks, and Cyril didn't want to anyway. Cyril said Boom-Boom was worth his place as striker, because he had scored five goals in one match.

I went up for the toss and I won it, and we lined up to start the match.

Mill Lane didn't look very big. They had black and yellow striped jerseys and their teacher came out with them and kept giving them instructions, but they didn't look like defending League champions. They had three or four players who were almost as titchy as ours.

We had all been reading the bulletin and we knew that McGaw and Beattie were the players who got most of the goals for Mill Lane, so we were looking out for them. The arrangement was that Daniel would pick up McGaw and I would shadow Beattie, and Cyril and John Deacon would tidy up behind us if things went wrong. We were playing a seven-man defence. We hoped that Mill Lane might turn out to be a two-man team, and if we could snuff the two men out we would have a chance of winning with breakaway goals.

They weren't a two-man team!

Their whole forward line could play. They were small, but they were well organized. Their teacher had trained them all to hold their positions, and they moved the ball about, and that meant that we were in trouble. They kept playing good balls down the wings. Three times their winger went past Joe Small, and Cyril had to come across to tackle. Cyril didn't make much of his tackles. The first time the winger beat Cyril to the ball but skyed his shot and put it behind for a goal kick. The second time John Deacon managed to intercept, and the third time the winner got to the touchline and pulled the ball back, but Terence came out and made a brilliant catch, taking the ball off McGaw's head as he was about to nod it home.

We were all pleased about that, because Terence had been having difficulty with crosses, and Mr Hope had had to help him. Mr Hope said that Terence's problem was that he was waiting for the ball to come to him, not attacking it, and players like Che Walls of Monk Noxon were able to come across him and beat him to the ball. Mr Hope told Terence he had to make use of the advantage his catching gave him over the attackers and take the ball *at the high point* where nobody else could reach it.

Here is Terence doing it against me in practice.

And here is what would have happened if Terence hadn't attacked the ball at the high point . . . Another Great Napper McCann Super Goal!

You can see that in both pictures I have timed my run to get in front of Terence. In the first picture, Terence comes off his line quickly, attacking the ball and taking it before I have any chance to get my head to it. In the second, with Terence hugging his line and waiting for an easy catch, I am able to get in front of him and head down into the net. Mr Hope put Harpur on the wing to take centres and he had me and Harry and Eddie taking turns to jump with Terence. That's the way it worked with near-posts balls. We did that, and then Mr Hope made Harpur mix in a few far-post balls as well, with Eddie making dummy runs to the near post and Harry coming in at the angle of the goal area.

'That's the most difficult ball of all for you to take, Terence,' Mr Hope said. 'You have to be forward in the goal, in case the winger slings the ball in for the near-post man, and then if he switches to the far post you have to back-pedal and come off your line at the same time. The man coming in on the far post has the advantage because he is running *towards* the ball, attacking it, and you are moving back. That's when you are likely to drop the ball if you attempt a catch. Best to punch clear, if you can.'

Our practice sessions had paid off because Terence had timed his run forward to the near post absolutely right.

'I'm going back to help Joe,' Daniel said, and he moved over to cover the winger. That meant that John Deacon had to take McGaw. It worked because Daniel managed to get a grip on the winger.

Mill Lane realized what was happening, and the next time Margolis, their little schemer, got the ball, he played it down the other flank where Beattie had gone on a run. I had gone with him, but Beattie managed to slip past me. He came haring in from the touchline into our penalty area and CRUNCH . . . Scuddy stopped him.

'Brilliant, Scuddy!' everybody shouted. Scuddy took the ball clean away from Beattie and played it up the wing to Jonathan. Jonathan got it, but he was afraid of being tackled in his plimsolls, so he just poked out his foot at it and the ball bobbed away from him.

Eddie went after it, along with their centre-half, Tony Scott. I played with Tony once, when we had a scratch team called Barnleck Wanderers, and I knew he was good. Eddie and Tony went racing down the wing together, and Tony got his foot to the ball and played it into touch. I was surprised that Eddie hadn't used his height and weight a bit more, because I thought he could have shoulder-charged Tony off the ball, but he didn't.

'Better luck next time, Boom-Boom!' I shouted.

Mill Lane came back on the attack. Margolis played a good ball to McGaw. Cyril went to cut it out, but McGaw flicked the ball inside towards Beattie. I nipped in and took the ball off his feet, and then I played it back to Cyril, who had doubled back to cover after McGaw's flick. Cyril had the ball on the edge of our area, and Terence called for it. Cyril stopped moving, and then he saw Rice, the winger, coming at him. Cyril booted the ball for touch. It was a panicky ball, and he mis-hit it. The ball ballooned off Rice and went up into the air over Cyril's head. Rice kept running on and Terence came crashing out of goal and made a super save, just nicking it off Rice's boot.

'Buck up, Cyril!' Mr Hope shouted.

Cyril looked down in the dumps.

Margolis got the ball again from Terence's kick. That was one of our problems. We had so many players back defending that there was no one to pick the ball up in midfield and feed it forward to Eddie. Margolis was hanging back picking up all the loose balls and laying passes on for Rice and McGaw and Beattie and the little winger that Daniel was marking. Eddie came back and chased Margolis this time, but the midfield man fooled him by back-heeling the ball to Paul Yates, one of their backs. Yates hit a long ball forward. I went for it and got my head to it, but the ball was just too high for me and instead of going forward it clipped off my head. Beattie came rushing in towards our goal and Terence came out desperately to narrow the angle. Beattie got the ball, drew Terence and shot. The ball beat Terence's dive and went flashing across our goal, but Scuddy managed to turn it away for a corner.

'That was a let-off!' Cyril said to me.

'Where were you?' I said.

'Beattie is *your* man,' Cyril said.

'You are supposed to cover me,' I said.

'I was covering the winger,' Cyril said.

'Daniel's taking the winger,' I said.

'What's Joe Small supposed to be doing, then?' said Cyril.

Margolis took the corner kick, but the ball went behind.

Terence took the goal kick. There was nobody to kick to in midfield, so he played a long ball towards the wing. Little Douglas King was standing there looking cold, even though he had a pullover on beneath his football jersey. When he saw the ball coming, he ran at it and wagged his leg. The ball bounced over his head. Paul Yates cleared it and Margolis beat Peter Scott and Joe Small to the bounce, and played it between Cyril and me.

'Yours!' shouted Cyril.

'Yours, Cyril!' I shouted.

Beattie went racing through between us and hit a real whizz-bang of a shot. Terence was coming out and he dived and got a hand to the ball, which glanced off his fingers and slammed against the post, and finished in the back of our net!

Goal!

1–0 to Mill Lane!

'Come on, Red Row! Sort yourselves out!' Mr Hope shouted from the touchline. 'Let's have the ball in their half of the field for a change, eh?'

It wasn't much use pumping the ball into their

half of the field, because Tony Scott or Yatesy or Margolis got it every time we did. Boom-Boom pulled back to help. He started tracking Margolis and shouted to Daniel to move up and be striker. Daniel stayed where he was, because we had seen what his winger could do! The first time Boom-Boom went for him, Margolis left him yards behind and got clear on the right, although he wasted the centre. The second time Boom-Boom BOOMED him!

'He's going to be sent off!' Joe Small said to me.

We thought he might be. There had already been a lot of fuss about rough play in the League, and we thought the ref might be waiting to pounce. Then we remembered who the ref was. The ref was John Deacon's dad! John Deacon's dad was doing it because the proper ref couldn't come. He'd got flu too. We didn't think John Deacon's dad would send anybody off, and he didn't.

'Up, up, upfield! Boomer!' Mr Hope shouted at Eddie. 'That's Rooney's man!'

'Is it?' said Daniel. 'Nobody told me.'

Then the half-time whistle went.

'What's the matter with you all?' Mr Hope said when we gathered round him at half-time. 'You're giving them the game on a plate.'

'They're all over us, Sir,' Daniel said. 'If it wasn't for Terence, we would be three or four goals down.'

'And Scuddy, Sir,' said Terence.

'Yes, well played, Scudamore!' said Mr Hope. 'Welcome back to the big time.'

Scuddy looked really pleased.

'At least you have been taking your man on,' said Mr Hope. 'There's a bit of bite in your tackles.'

Nobody said anything.

'Well?' said Mr Hope.

'You told us not to lay into them, Sir,' said Cyril. It was a joke, really, because right through the first half Cyril hadn't got near enough to anyone to lay into them. Any time anyone came near him, he booted the ball away or left it to Daniel and me. We had been getting into a terrible muddle.

'Tackle as hard as you like, so long as it is fair!' said Mr Hope. 'Anyway, I don't know why you are all holding back in your own half. This team has had ninety per cent of the play, and all they've got to show for it is a goal which you handed them on a plate. You haven't started playing yet!'

'It's all the little ones, Sir,' I said. 'They can't play. When we pass the ball to them, they lose it.'

'At least the little ones are trying,' said Mr Hope. 'I said defend for the first five minutes until you had sorted things out, not for the whole game.'

'You mean we should attack, Sir?' said Cyril.

'Yes. Attack, attack, ATTACK! You've got to open out and take a few risks. Get at them! They're looking good because you are *letting* them look good. And tackle, tackle, TACKLE!'

'I think we should put somebody on Margolis, Sir,' I said. 'He's running the middle of the field, and their strikers are feeding off him. I reckon we could stop them by stopping him, Sir.'

'You're elected, Napper!' he said. 'Go hunt Margolis.'

Mr Deacon blew his whistle, and we went back on to the field. We arranged that Scuddy would take Rice and Cyril would take Beattie and John Deacon would take McGaw, leaving Daniel to mark the winger and try to get forward if he could to help me. I was to take Margolis on and try to get a few runs at goal myself, or feed Eddie if I couldn't get up.

'Hunt the ball, Napper!' Mr Hope shouted at me as they kicked off, and that is what I started doing. But it was one thing to hunt it and another thing to do something with it.

Tony Scott was lying tight up on Eddie, so I tried playing long balls for Eddie to run on to. The trouble was that Eddie wasn't quick enough, and he was so worried about being sent off for fouling and being barred from the team by Mr Hope that he didn't challenge hard either. Each time I played the ball past them, Tony picked it up and fed Margolis, and then I had to chase after him.

That bit worked well, anyway. Margolis was good as long as he was left alone, but I quickly found he didn't like being tackled. He started drifting out towards the wing. GREAT!

I tried laying the ball short for Eddie, but his control was so bad that that wasn't much use, because Tony was able to cut him out. There was nobody else to pass to. Jonathan Ramsey couldn't kick the ball without his boots and that left only little Douglas. Douglas was running about trying to play, but Paul Yates was too big for him. I like Paul Yates. He's a good player. If it had been Knocker Lewis, he would have banged Douglas out of the game, the way he once did to Dribbler.

'Give us a decent ball, Napper!' Eddie moaned.

'Do something with it!' I shouted back.

Margolis started to come back into it. He disappeared when I first started tackling, but McGaw and Beattie started shouting at him, so he came in and thought he would have another go. I picked him up just inside our half, and I thought I would go in really hard to make him remember that the easy times were over. I tried a Napper McCann Super Slide-tackle. He hopped out of it and left me sprawling! We would have been in trouble if Joe Small hadn't got in the way and cleared the ball.

Margolis gave me a big grin as he ran back. The next time he got the ball I closed him down again, and then I thought I would back-pedal so that the defence could cover. The trouble was that Margolis used my backing-off to pick up speed, and he finally played a deadly ball into the area, which McGaw flicked against the upright with the side of his boot. The ball went out for a goal kick to us.

'Nail him, Napper!' John Deacon said.

'ATTACK! ATTACK! ATTACK!' Mr Hope was yelling at me from the side of the pitch. How could I be in two places at once?

Margolis had started playing again, and Mill Lane were getting more confident. Tony Scott came off Eddie and moved up because no balls were coming through the middle any more. That was because I was too busy with Margolis to do any attacking.

'Gaps!' Cyril said to me.

Boom-Boom saw it too. John Deacon won a loose ball and clipped it forward over Tony Scott's head, right into Eddie's path. Eddie got it and put his head down and charged. I reckon their goalie must have been petrified by the sight of Eddie, because he stood there on his line and Eddie got to the edge of the area and walloped the ball and it banged into the back of the net!

1–1!

We were level, with almost the only attacking chance we had had!

The way Eddie carried on, you would have thought he had just won us the World Cup.

'Cut it out, Boomer!' Mr Hope shouted from the line. We didn't mind how much Eddie boomed, if only he got some goals.

John Deacon came away with the ball, forgetting all about being a defender. He played it wide to Daniel Rooney, who had come up from the back.

Daniel took it in his stride, and flicked it past McGaw, who'd moved back to mark him. It beat Eddie Boomer and Tony Scott and went towards Jonathan Ramsey, who was on the half-way line. Jonathan couldn't hit it far, but he managed to get it to me. I controlled it, and found Margolis coming at me.

'My turn!' I thought.

He lunged in and I nutmegged him! I put the ball straight through his legs. Margolis went down, and I was on my way. It was the first run at goal I'd had in the match.

Yatesy came at me. I feinted to go inside, and then booted the ball past him on the wing. Yatesy bought it! I got through and fired across a great centre.

Eddie Boomer was storming in. He took off for a diving header and crashed the ball at their goal, but the Mill Lane goalie made a Wonder Save, shoving the ball up in the air. The ball banged off the post and came out again to Jonathan Ramsey, who'd run on up the field. Jonathan trapped it. Their goalie came charging out at him. Jonathan poked his foot at it and his shot hit the goalie and bounced towards me. I lashed a Superdrive from the edge of the area, right for the left-hand corner of the empty net. I think it would have gone in, but Eddie Boomer helped it by sticking out his boot as he lay on the ground. The ball banged past Tony Scott for a Magnificent Goal!

GOAL!

2–1 to Red Row.

We were winning

Mr Deacon blew his whistle, and pointed for a free kick.

'Offside!' he said.

'Augh, ref!' I shouted.

'There was a man on the line!' Eddie shouted.

Mr Deacon ignored us, and ran back up the pitch.

'That was a good goal,' I said. 'We were robbed. How could it be offside? There was a man on the line, and Eddie knocked it past him.'

I found out later that I was wrong. Mr Hope showed us all how. 'The offside law says *two* men, Napper,' he said. 'One defender *and the goalkeeper*. You ought to know that.'

The goalie had unintentionally played Eddie offside.

'What if Napper's shot had gone in without Eddie touching it, Sir?' Terence asked.

'Then it would be up to the referee,' said Mr Hope. 'He would have had to decide whether or not he thought Eddie was interfering with play.'

It didn't matter anyway, because Eddie *had* played the ball and he was offside.

Margolis got the ball from the free kick and I went after him again, but Joe Small did too. We thought that two of us might be better than one. Joe went in first and I held back. When Margolis beat Joe, I was able to slide in and crash the ball into touch. Margolis shrugged and walked away. He didn't even get the ball back for the throw-in.

'Good play!' shouted Mr Hope.

Mill Lane were getting tired. We had started playing, coming at them, and now we were on top. We kept piling attack after attack on their goal, but all the attacks were coming from long balls to Eddie, and Tony Scott was still winning most of them.

Then they got away down the left. Paul Yates came up from the back to make the extra man and got clear. Scuddy came off Rice to take him and Yatesy squared the ball inside. Peter Scott and Cyril went for it together. Peter got there first. He was moving towards our goal and for once in his life he hit the ball really hard – into his own goal!

Terence could only blink as the ball whizzed past him!

Mill Lane went bananas. They'd been playing badly and had let us back into it, and now suddenly they had struck back with what looked like the winner! They were 2–1 up, and time was running out.

'Great goal, Pete!' Terence said, fishing the ball out of the back of the net.

Peter looked sick!

Tony Scott started clapping his hands and shouting at their players to come back and tighten things up. Most of them did, except Margolis. He was right out of it.

Then we got a free kick and I gave Secret Sign Number Five for the Small Special. The idea was that Daniel Rooney would make a near-post run, diverting the defenders, and I would switch the ball to the far post, where Cyril would head it in. It relied on Cyril coming up from the back and making his run late.

Number Five isn't complicated, but then dead-ball plans don't need to be. If you make them complicated, they go wrong! The whole point of having them is that you know exactly what you are going to do *before* you take the kick. The defending side have to work out what is happening *as it is happening*, and that often means that they make mistakes – like falling for decoy runs.

Here is how Number Five, the Small Special, is meant to work:

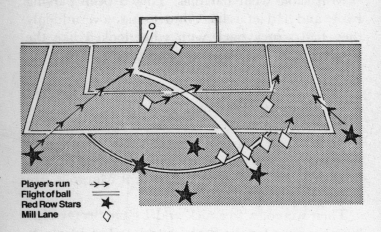

Player's run	→→
Flight of ball	══
Red Row Stars	★
Mill Lane	◇

We worked it well. Cyril met the ball with his head and zonked it straight into the back of the Mill Lane net!

BRILLIANT GOAL!

That's what we thought, but Boom-Boom was offside again!

'Hard luck, boys!' Mr Hope shouted. 'Watch the play, Boomer! Don't get caught!'

Eddie didn't look pleased. He had run miles in the game, banging about and trying to find a way past Tony Scott, who was too good for him. I felt sorry for old Boom-Boom because everybody was going on about him being offside, and forgetting the really good goal he'd got.

Then we got a corner.

I grabbed the ball to take it because I had had a good idea. We hadn't been practising with Terence all week for nothing.

Eddie guessed what I was doing.

He positioned himself for a near-post run.

I hit a high near-post ball, and Eddie came in across the keeper. The keeper hesitated and Eddie rammed his head in . . .

GOAL!

Exactly as we had practised. It was a great goal, and we all felt as pleased as Punch because it had worked out so well.

2–2!

Mill Lane had had it. We kept coming on and attacking, and they were just kicking anywhere. Then I got the ball about twenty yards from goal. Margolis made a half-hearted attempt to tackle, but I skipped out of it and squared the ball to Cyril, who had come forward. Cyril went on a run and Paul Yates came to get him. Cyril booted the ball on and Eddie came bashing across with Tony Scott. Tony got there first, but Eddie spoiled him with a good tackle and the ball ran loose on the edge of the area to Douglas King. Douglas was so surprised that he didn't know what to do. But he soon woke up. Douglas pushed the ball forward and the goalie shouted, '*Mine!*', and came rushing out of goal to drop on it. But instead of dropping on it he fumbled it, and the ball bounced back towards Douglas, and Douglas banged it into the net!

GOAL!

The whistle went before we could even kick off again!

Everybody went mad. They were all laughing and cheering and running about, and Boom-Boom was trying to lift Douglas in the air and Cyril was thumping Terence!

'You were dead lucky, Napper,' Joe Fish said, coming up to me. 'They should have finished you off in the first half.'

'I know,' I said.

'Good thing you didn't meet their full team,' he said.

'What?'

'They had a lot of kids off with flu,' he said. 'You should have had a go at them earlier. Your lot looked as if they were afraid of Mill Lane in the first half. Soon as you started attacking in the second half, they crumpled like a wet paper bag.'

I told Cyril about it when we were changing.

'So what?' Cyril said. 'We had men short too and we won, didn't we? We'd have won if both teams had been full strength, I reckon. They weren't much. I don't know how they got to be League champions.'

'They were League champions last year,' I said. 'This is probably a different team.'

'We're going to win it this time,' Cyril said. 'That gives us four points out of six, and if we win our next two games we'll have eight, and that ought to be enough to win it.'

'Yeah,' I said, doubtfully.

'I *told* everybody we would,' said Cyril. 'Didn't I? I told everybody I know. So we've got to win it, haven't we?'

PRIMARY SCHOOLS LEAGUE

BULLETIN NO. 4

THIRD-ROUND RESULTS:

Red Row 3   Mill Lane 2
St Gabriel's 12   Langland 0
Monk Noxon 2   John Abbott 3

RED ROW V. MILL LANE

Both teams were under-strength due to the flu bug. Mill Lane failed to capitalize on a good performance in the first half. Red Row moved into top gear after the interval and narrowly scraped home at the finish, King snatching a winner in the closing seconds. Boomer (2) and King scored for Red Row, Beattie and Scott (o.g.) for Mill Lane. Our thanks to Mr Clement Deacon for stepping in to referee at short notice. Didn't he do well!

ST GABRIEL'S V. LANGLAND

A strong St Gabriel's side completely outclassed the youthful Langland. Bridges (4), Cleland (3), Collins (3), Lewis and Fish were the goalscorers.

MONK NOXON V. JOHN ABBOTT

John Abbott moved to the top of the League with a narrow victory over the fancied Monk Noxon side in a hotly contested game, where no quarter was given or asked for! John Abbott's Gowland had an outstanding game and notched a hat-trick. Peirce and Ryan replied for Monk Noxon.

LEAGUE TABLE

	P	W	D	L	F	A	Pts
John Abbott	3	2	1	0	10	7	5
St Gabriel's	3	1	2	0	18	6	4
Red Row	3	2	0	1	10	8	4
Monk Noxon	3	1	1	1	10	6	3
Mill Lane	3	1	0	2	10	7	2
Langland	3	0	0	3	1	25	0

FOURTH-ROUND FIXTURES:
John Abbott v. Red Row
Mill Lane v. St Gabriel's
Langland v. Monk Noxon

John Abbott, one point clear at the top of the table, face a stiff challenge from newcomers Red Row, who may find the task too much for them. High-scoring St Gabriel's will expect to maintain their challenge at the expense of the disappointing Mill Lane, and Langland cannot be expected to hold Monk Noxon, who will be anxious to prove that their defeat by John Abbott in the previous round was only a temporary setback.

The Committee is still concerned at the level of rough play in the competition and, with this in mind, it has been decided to institute a Sub-committee to consider ways and means of dealing with the problem. Each school participating in this season's competition will be entitled to a voting place on this Sub-committee, whose recommendations will be considered and, we hope, implemented before the commencement of the next competition.

D. W. Overend (Secretary)

6. The Top-Secret Meeting

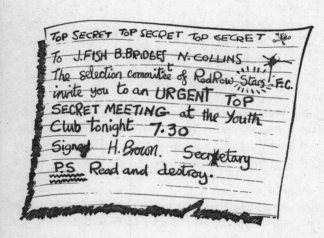

TOP SECRET TOP SECRET TOP SECRET

To J.FISH B.BRIDGES N.COLLINS
The selection committee of RedRow Stars F.C.
invite you to an URGENT TOP
SECRET MEETING at the Youth
Club tonight 7.30
Signed H.Brown. Secretary
P.S. Read and destroy.

'What's this about?' Joe Fish said, putting our Top Secret Meeting Message down on the coffee table.

'You were supposed to eat that,' Cyril said. 'Look. It says, "Read and destroy".'

'You eat it then, Cyril,' said Neil Collins. 'You look like you eat anything.'

'Shut up, Cyril,' Terence said.

'Well, what's it about?' said Joe.

'We're playing John Abbott on Saturday in the League,' Terence said.

'We've already played them,' Neil said. 'So what?'

'They'll pulverize you,' Bob Bridges said.

'If they do, you've no chance of winning the League,' I said.

'What?'

'If John Abbott beat us, they'll have seven points, right? And if you beat Mill Lane, you'll have six. You play us in your last game. *If* you beat us, you can get eight. John Abbott are going to get nine.'

'Why?' said Bob.

Joe Fish got it before we could explain. 'John Abbott's last game is against Langland,' he said. 'They're bound to win *that*.'

'In other words,' I said, 'if John Abbott beat us, they win the League. But if *we* beat *them*, we'll have six points and you'll have six points and nobody else can do better than five. Then the team that wins when we play each other wins the League.'

'*If* you beat John Abbott,' said Bob Bridges. 'Some hopes! Wait'll Baldie gets you!'

'Who's Baldie?'

'Baldwin. He's a big bald kid. He kicked Neil out of the game against us, didn't he, Neil? And he got Zico Ryan. Zico had to go off at half-time when they played Monk Noxon. That's why Monk Noxon lost.'

'Didn't you see the bulletin?' said Joe. 'All those

bits about rough teams? That was John Abbott. All the teachers have been going on about them.'

I looked at Terence. 'We thought that was about *us*,' Terence said.

Joe Fish grinned. 'You wait till you play the Abbotts!' he said. 'They've kicked their way to the top of the League, and now it looks as if they'll win it.'

'Not if you help us,' I said.

'Eh?'

'That's what the Top-Secret Meeting is for,' I said. 'You've played them. You tell us who their danger men are and we *might* beat them. See?'

'But —' Neil said.

'We're not going to help you lot win the League!' Bob Bridges said.

'If we beat the Abbotts, *you* have a chance of winning it *yourselves*,' Terence said. 'If *we* lose, *you* lose.'

The Stringy Pants thought about it.

'You're right!' Joe Fish said. 'Top-Secret Information on John Abbott's football team coming up!'

Joe and Neil and Bob Bridges told us all about John Abbott, and we told Mr Hope at training, although we didn't tell him who we'd got the Top-Secret Information from.

'They're dead rough, Sir!' Cyril said. 'This Baldie goes round breaking legs.'

'I don't think anybody has had a leg broken yet, Cyril,' said Mr Hope. Cyril goes on a lot about broken legs because his was once broken.

'What are we going to do about it, Sir?'

'Play football!' said Mr Hope. 'They can concentrate on rough-house tactics if they want to. You play the ball and let the ref worry about the rules.'

Everybody was looking worried, particularly the small ones.

'Come on,' said Mr Hope. 'Practice match.'

We started our practice match and Mr Hope refereed, but half-way through he stopped the match.

'I don't know about breaking legs,' he said, 'but there's some pretty odd tackling going on here!'

Then he got hold of Eddie Boomer.

'Arms! Arms! Arms!' he said. 'You're going in like a windmill, Boomer. Arms all over the place. And when you don't go in like a windmill, you're like a cart-horse stung by a bee! I don't think you mean to foul people, but you'll have to watch it or it won't be the John Abbott players who are in trouble with the ref! Isn't that right, Haxwell?'

Harry just grinned. When we first started playing, Harry used to give away lots of fouls, but now he doesn't.

Then Mr Hope showed us what Eddie was doing wrong.

'You've got to get the ball and not the man, Boomer,' said Mr Hope. 'You can't stick your arms in his face, or bang him in the back, or go lunging in two-footed to break his leg, or tackle late. Keep your elbows out of his ribs and don't, for goodness' sake, try to walk through people!'

Mr Hope got Cyril to show Eddie how to do it properly. He took Eddie and Cyril down behind the bike shed, and he made Cyril tackle Eddie again and again and again.

'Go on, Cyril! *Harder!*' said Mr Hope.

Cyril did it, and when we played the second half of the practice match he went round crunching everybody. Once he saw that he could take on Eddie Boomer, our biggest player, Cyril forgot all about his bad leg. We all knew that he could tackle, but he hadn't been doing it properly since he hurt his leg, which is probably why Mr Hope picked on Cyril to take on Eddie.

'No Scottie and Mark in the team this week, so see you do that on Saturday,' Mr Hope said to Cyril. 'You've got to start making decisions at the back, Small. You run the show. Right?'

Cyril looked dead chuffed!

'What about Gowland?' I said.

'Who?' said Mr Hope.

'Nine goals in three games, and they've only scored ten altogether,' said Harpur. Joe had told us a lot about Gowland and the two wingers.

'Boomer has scored seven,' said Mr Hope. 'Haven't you, Boomer?'

Eddie looked pleased. The problem was that we all knew he had missed trillions as well. Most of his goals were against Langland, and they didn't count.

'Don't get fussed about their centre-forward,' said Mr Hope. 'Let them get fussed about us. If they put their best man on to Boomer, that means all the more chances for the rest of you. Boomer draws him out of defence, and you move in! Something from you, Napper, or have you forgotten about scoring goals? Rooney? Brown? Haxwell? If Boomer can make a gap by taking out one of their best defenders, you ought to be able to profit by it – if Boomer stays onside, that is!'

'Sounds great,' said Harpur afterwards. 'But can we do it?'

'Course we can!' said Cyril.

7. Red Row Stars v. John Abbott

PRIMARY SCHOOLS LEAGUE:
FOURTH ROUND
John Abbott P.S. v. Red Row P.S.
Referee: B. Malone
Venue: John Abbott P.S. Playing Fields, Warne

The Selection Committee had a lot of arguments picking the team to play the League leaders, John Abbott, in the match that looked as if it might decide the championship. This is the team we picked:

T. Prince

S. Rodgers   J. Small

C. Small

J. Deacon   H. Haxwell

N. McCann (Capt.)   H. Brown

D. Rooney   E. Boomer   D. Wilson

Substitute P. Scott

Trainer Mr Hope

Travelling Official Miss E. Fellows

It wasn't like our usual team, with backs and midfield men and strikers. Mr Hope said it was the 'W' formation, the way lots of teams used to play before there were strikers and midfield men. He said we should try it because it meant that all our players would know precisely what they had to do. I think his main idea was to get Cyril to take responsibility for the defence and to make sure that Harpur and I kept going forward. He said fancy systems were muddling us up.

'You are inside-*forwards* now, not midfield men!' said Mr Hope. 'That doesn't mean you don't defend, but it does mean that your main job is to get *forward* quickly and help the two wingers and the centre-forward. John and Harry are wing half-*backs*. That means their main job is to *stop* the opposition. Cyril is centre-half. He is responsible for anything that happens in the centre of the defence. No calling to other people to take on your men, Cyril! If it's in the middle, it's up to you! The backs pick up the wingers. Rooney, Boomer and Wilson, you stay upfield. Napper and Harpur will be playing balls forward for you and closing up from behind to help you. Right? Everybody know what they have to do? Do it!'

'Why is it called the "W" formation, Sir?' said Cyril.

Mr Hope showed us. It was like two 'W's.

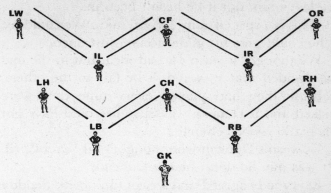

'Man. United don't play like that,' said Cyril.

'Manchester United don't get confused about who is doing what on the field, Cyril,' said Mr Hope. 'I want you to play this way to stop the confusion, all right? The way you played last week, it looked to me as if nobody knew what they were doing, or supposed to be doing.'

We thought it sounded a good idea to get rid of all the muddle we'd been having, so we picked our team to play that way.

The biggest argument we had picking the team was about P. Scott. At first we thought we had to have Peter in it because St Gabriel's had told us that John Abbott had the hardest-tackling team in the League, and we should pick our toughest players. Then we had to think about who we were going to leave out. It was Scuddy, or Joe, or Duncan.

'Duncan hasn't been *in*,' said Terence. 'How can we leave him out if he hasn't been in?'

'This is a special game,' Cyril said. 'We could see if he could miss his piano lesson, just once.'

We thought it wasn't a bad idea, but in the end we decided that it wouldn't be fair to the others, because they had played every time they were picked and if Duncan was fussy he could have got his piano lessons changed.

'It wasn't Duncan who thought of it,' said Cyril. 'It was me. So don't blame Duncan.'

Everybody agreed that we couldn't leave Scuddy out after the way he played against Mill Lane, so it was Joe Small.

We thought about dropping Joe.

'I want Joe in,' said Harpur. 'I'd rather have Joe than Peter any day!'

So we picked Joe Small for left-back.

P. Scott wasn't pleased!

'Amn't I in it?' said Douglas King when he saw the team sheet on the noticeboard. He thought he would be in the team because he had scored the winning goal against Mill Lane. We told him he was too little. Mr Hope said he could be Official Assistant Trainer and he came along to Warne with us. He brought his boots with him, just in case. Jonathan Ramsey never said anything. I don't think he thought he would be picked.

Mr Hope and Miss Fellows drove us up to Warne in their cars and we went into John Abbott School to get changed. Their team was waiting for us, and they all looked at us and we looked at them.

'Which one is Boomer?' one of them said.

They thought Eddie was our star player. I didn't mind, because I knew it would give me a chance to be our Secret Weapon. Eddie just walked by, whistling.

'He's BIG!' one of their players said.

'We'll get you, Boomer!' somebody shouted. Then Mr Hope came down the corridor with our kit and they cleared off.

We changed in one of their classrooms. Somebody had been chalking things on the board. Things like ABBOTTS ARE CHAMPIONS and BALDIE EATS BOOMERS!

We knew all about Baldie! Joe Fish had told us for our Top-Secret Dossier. Joe said he was John Abbott's biggest player. They stuck him at the back and his job was to snuff out star attackers.

'He kicked me,' Neil Collins said. 'Then he went after Bob Bridges. The whole team is like that. They go in like tanks. But Baldie is worst.'

'He'd better keep away from me, that's all,' Eddie said. The other players we had to watch for were Gowland, who got all the goals, their Captain, Jensen, and their two wingers, Dubray and Roper.

'I reckon you could beat them if they don't put you off with their tackling,' said Joe Fish.

Their pitch was right behind their school, and the whole school turned up. The supporters were playing football in the goalmouths, and their teachers had to chase them so we could get one of the nets. When the John Abbott players came out, the supporters all started shouting and cheering and waving flags. The only support we had was Mr Hope, Miss Fellows and Douglas King and the bucket. Peter Scott doesn't count because he was our sub.

They had proper goals with nets, and also corner flags. John Abbott were dressed in white shirts and shorts. They had three footballs and they looked very professional. They went down the far end and started kicking about, all except a big one with no hair. He stopped about half-way down the pitch and stood looking at us.

'Reckon they're not much cop,' Eddie said loudly, and he started bouncing up and down to show how fit he was.

I wasn't so sure. I didn't like the look of Baldie!

I lost the toss and they chose ends, so we got kick-off. I lined up beside Eddie, trying not to think about being kicked.

We kicked off, and straight away we put our plan into action.

Our plan was to spend the first five or ten minutes making John Abbott believe that Eddie was the only forward we had got. Harpur and I would lie back and pump long balls forward for Eddie to chase. We thought that Baldie would spot it and decide that Eddie was the danger man. He would close up on Eddie, and then Eddie would start to wander out of the middle as if he was looking for space, hoping to draw Baldie with him. Joe Fish and Neil said that the rest of the John Abbott defence was rubbish, apart from Jensen, and Jensen was always going off upfield.

'Baldie will clobber Boomer,' Bob Bridges said, but we weren't worried. We thought it was one thing for Baldie to clobber little players like Zico Ryan and Neil Collins and Margolis of Mill Lane, and quite another to take on Boom-Boom. We reckoned Boom-Boom was big enough to take care of himself.

'Don't you clobber him, Eddie!' Terence warned. 'That's not the plan. Get up if he knocks you down, keep on playing and draw him out of the middle. If he gets mad, that's brilliant! The crosser he gets, the more he'll chase you!' We thought that if Baldie went Boom-Boom hunting, there would be plenty of space for the rest of us to move into!

Eddie and Baldie got mixed up straight away. First, Eddie got the ball half-way inside their half, and Baldie tried to kick chunks out of him. The ref's whistle went.

Eddie got up and grinned at Baldie, then he walked away.

Free kick to us.

'Test the keeper out?' said Harpur, because Bob had told us that the keeper was shaky on high balls.

He hit a long floater into the area, and Eddie and Baldie went for it. The keeper came out too. He got up above them and held his catch, coolly and confidently.

'Maybe St Gabriel's were kidding us?' Harpur said as he moved back.

The keeper threw the ball clear, and all the John Abbott supporters cheered him.

Eddie and Baldie got up from the ground, and Baldie said something to Eddie. Eddie just grinned.

The next time Eddie got the ball, Baldie hammered him. It was a good tackle and it sent Eddie sprawling on his face.

'Move off him, Boomer!' Mr Hope shouted. 'Pop up all over the place.'

That is what Eddie was trying to do. He got away on the left and Baldie and a kid called Bennett both went for him. They both arrived at once, and we got a free kick for sandwiching.

Harpur gave Secret Sign Number Five again, the Small Special. We had been working on our Secret Sign plans all week, trying to sort them out. The big problem was that Eddie kept getting offside, and everybody had told him not to.

We all went forward into the area. Jensen, their Captain, took me, and Eddie and Baldie were jostling each other on the edge of the area. Baldie had followed Eddie out of the box, which left them short of cover in the middle.

Harpur came up to take the kick, and Daniel

started his run. His marker went with him. Harpur clipped the ball, and there was Cyril coming in from behind to rocket the ball into the back of the net for a brilliant first goal!

1–0 to Red Row Stars!

We were a goal up and the game had only just started.

John Abbott didn't know what had hit them! They started kicking the ball anywhere, which meant we got it. First, Dribbler had a go down the wing and sent over a high centre that the goalie missed but their full-back headed off the line, and then Eddie got away down the right and was tackled high by Baldie. The ball went into touch, but what Baldie hadn't reckoned on was Eddie's weight. The two of them went down under the impact of the tackle, and Baldie was underneath. He was winded and their trainer had to come on.

The ref gave another free kick to us.

Harpur took it and played the ball high for Eddie. Eddie got up above Baldie, who didn't look too keen on going for the ball. Eddie's header thumped against the bar with the keeper beaten. One of their players kicked it clear, and their Captain, Jensen, got the ball.

Jensen was trying to cool them down. He got the ball, stopped and held it. I went in, and he played the ball past me, towards the gap between John Deacon and Cyril, where Gowland was heading.

'Mine, John!' Cyril yelled, and he headed the ball out for a throw-in.

'Well done, Cyril!' Mr Hope shouted. We were all pleased. It was a fifty-fifty ball between our two players, but Cyril had made sure it was his. If he went on like that, we reckoned he could button up the middle!

Their winger, Dubray, got the ball from the throw-in. Scuddy was late going out to him, and he fired the ball across our area, where Gowland got it with his back towards goal and Cyril closing up on him fast.

Gowland took the ball on his chest, and then he tried a bicycle kick from about the penalty spot which was supposed to be a shot. He nearly hit the corner flag.

'Watch him!' Terence shouted. Terence had got

the message. Gowland was a Hit-Everything Merchant. We thought that might not be a bad thing for us. Terence is a good goalie who keeps on his toes. He isn't easy to beat with snap shots. Gowland could have played the ball back to Jensen, who had slipped me and was moving clear, or turned it back to his inside man, who would have had room to send Roper clear on the other flank, but Gowland wasn't that sort of player. Shoot-on-sight was all he was interested in. Joe had told us the same thing. It worked well when the rest of the John Abbott team had softened up the opposition and they were on all-out attack, but he still missed more often than he was on target.

John Deacon got the ball and played it forward for Daniel. Daniel lost control, and the running battle between Eddie and Baldie arrived on the spot. They were so busy banging each other that neither of them got the ball and I was able to nip on to it. I took it to the edge of the area and laid it back for Harpur, who was following up. Harpur blasted it and the goalie made a good save, although he fumbled the ball and had to be quick to take it off Dribbler's feet.

We were well on top!

'Attack! Attack! Attack!' Mr Hope was shouting, and Douglas King was bouncing up and down on the line.

Jensen played a neat ball down the wing to Dubray, who beat Scuddy again. John Deacon came back and Dubray nutmegged him, but he lost control and Scuddy got back to turn the ball for a corner. It would have been more dangerous if Dubray had centred after he beat Scuddy and before our team could recover.

Dubray took the corner. Cyril went for the ball and Gowland was with him, but Terence called and came flying off his line. He plucked the ball off Gowland's head and landed almost on the penalty spot. It looked dangerous because he was so far from his goal, but he had read the cross perfectly.

'Punch if you are in trouble, Terence,' Mr Hope shouted, but I think Terence was right to catch the ball. If he had punched out, he would have been caught off his line, wide open to anyone collecting and lobbing the ball back.

Terence got up and kicked the ball down the middle. Boom-Boom went for it with Baldie breathing down his neck. Boom-Boom got his head to it and they both went over in a bundle. The header came to me and I hit it first time to the edge of the area, where Daniel had outsprinted Bennett. Daniel was going to bash it home into the net when Bennett stuck out his leg and Daniel went sprawling!

PENALTY!

It looked a real cert., but the ref didn't give it. He signalled for a goal kick!

The goalie took the goal kick, grinning all over his face.

106

John Abbott had had a let-off and it really bucked them up. They went on to the attack using Roper and Dubray. Dubray was having a real battle with Scuddy and John Deacon; but the trouble was, that left John's man unmarked, so I had to pick him up, and that left Jensen free. Jensen was a real danger.

Terence made two great saves, one after the other. The first was when Jensen hit a long ball into the area and Gowland got above Cyril and headed for the far post. Terence got a hand to it and pushed it round for a corner. Then the corner came across. Terence misjudged it and tried to turn it over. He flicked the ball against the bar and the ball came down. Gowland arrived to smash it in and Terence just managed to get there at the same time! Gowland ended up in the back of the net, but Terence managed to hold on.

'Come on, John Abbott!' Jensen shouted. 'They're on the run.'

Gowland got clear on the left and smacked in a shot that nearly broke the post in two. It was from outside the area, but Gowland hit it so hard that Terence never had a chance. The ball came back to Roper, who blazed it over the bar when it would have been easier to score – so at least I wasn't the only one who could miss chances!

'Open out, Red Row!' Mr Hope shouted. He was looking worried. He started to shout at me to go forward.

'You're hiding yourself, Napper! What's the matter? Get up there! Attack. Take Jensen on. Keep him in his own half!'

'You'd better go up, Napper,' Harpur said. 'There's no one to pass to.'

He was right. Daniel had faded out of the game, Dribbler had never really got into it, and Eddie and Baldie were cancelling each other out. Neither of them could get clear of the other. It was exactly what we had planned to happen, except that Harpur and I were supposed to come forward to pick up the loose balls, and we hadn't been doing it.

I moved forward, and when Harpur next got the ball he played it forward to Eddie. Eddie and Baldie banged together and the ball broke to me. I got clear of the full back and hit in a Real Napper McCann Super Screecher, which beat the goalie all ends up and smacked into the side of the net – on the WRONG side of the post!

No goal.

Mr Hope had his head in his hands!

Then we got a corner kick. Dribbler took it and played a near-post ball. Eddie went for it, the keeper stayed, and Eddie beat Baldie and headed against the bar. I came blazing in for the rebound – and missed it!

The ball was cleared upfield, and Gowland showed us why he was the top scorer in the League. He picked up a through ball from one of their midfielders, left Cyril sprawling, cut inside our area and unleashed a terrific drive that almost blew the back of our net away.

1–1!

The John Abbott fans on the line almost went mad! They'd gone one down early on, then they'd started to wear us down with their hard tackling, and now they had snatched an equalizer almost on the stroke of half-time.

We got one more chance. Eddie had moved out of the middle, with Baldie tagging after him. Harpur spotted it and played a long ball over both of them for me to move on to. The goalie started to come out of goal and I could have lobbed him, but I reckoned it was smarter to play the ball across to Daniel, who would have an open goal. I mis-hit the ball, and Bennett got it and cleared for a corner.

'Shoot, Napper!' Mr Hope shouted.

'Sounds like a good idea to me,' said Daniel. 'Anybody got a gun?'

Half-time, 1–1.

'You're doing it again!' said Mr Hope. 'You're a much better team than they are. You showed that in the first quarter of the game. But you're letting them get on top of you. You're so worried about defending that you don't seem to realize how weak they are! Everything's going right up front for you . . . Jensen's shoving up out of position, and the big centre-half doesn't realize there is anybody else on our team except Boomer! The further he gets from the middle, the more room for the rest of you to nip in! Their goalie can't hold his shots. Their backs are slow! Attack them! Start going forward! Wilson, get into the game! Well done, Cyril Small! Best game you've played all season. Rooney? You're not in the game, Son.'

'Nobody's passing to me!' muttered Daniel.

'Then go and get the ball yourself!'

Daniel shrugged.

'Napper?'

'Not my day, Sir.'

'This half, you go forward and you stay forward, and you do what you do best! Score goals! Shoot! Take risks! I don't want to see you defending. That's just hiding from your real job in the team because you have missed a few. Don't mark Jensen. Let him mark you!'

I nodded.

'Some of them are trying to break legs, Sir!' Harry said.

'Well? It isn't working, is it? Their whole game is built round the two big boys, Gowland and the boy at the back.'

'Baldie,' said Eddie.

'That's right. They're chucking their weight around, so are some of the others. Let them! Don't get ruffled. They can't kick you and the ball. Keep your tempers and you'll win. Mix it and you'll lose. This team is strong, but they can't play football!'

Gowland lined up to kick off. He was already shouting to his mates on the touchline about what he was going to do in the second half.

The game started and they went at us. Harry was knocked down by Roper, Cyril got in a clash with Gowland that nearly flattened both of them, and Baldie had another go at cutting Eddie's legs off at the knees.

'Easy, Eddie!' I shouted when Eddie got up. Eddie glared at Baldie. Baldie glared back. He was following Eddie all round the park.

Dribbler was really dumped by one of their backs, and Jensen had a go at me.

'Hey!' I said.

'What's the matter?' he said. 'Gone soft?'

I got my own back.

Daniel got the ball on the wing. He saw me moving and played in a long ball that Baldie should have cut out. Baldie was too far over, crowding Eddie, so he missed it. I got the ball as it swept past him, and I played it forward and went after it with Jensen closing on me. He lunged in two-footed and I hopped his tackle and headed for the goal. I reckon if he'd tried to play the ball he might have got it!

I got control and slipped the ball inside. Eddie and Baldie arrived at the same moment in the area. Eddie stretched for the ball, and Baldie nudged him in the back. Eddie went down for the ninety-ninth time in the match, bang in the middle of the area!

PENALTY!

This time, the ref gave it!

'I'll take it if you like,' Eddie said.

I wished he hadn't said it. Taking penalties was my job.

I shook my head.

'You blast it, then!' said Eddie.

'To his right, Napper,' said Daniel.

'Just burst the net, Napper,' said Harpur.

'He never misses, do you, Napper?' said Harry

I put the ball on the spot. They were all full of advice, but they didn't have to do it. I had already made up my mind what I was going to do. Low down, inside the left-hand post.

I walked back and faced the goalie.

He was chewing something. He crouched on his line, his eyes fixed on the ball.

'Ready, Son?' the ref asked.

The ref blew his whistle.

I ran up. The goalie swayed left just as I was hitting the ball and I thought I'd switch it to his other side, so I did. I belted a Napper McCann Super Shot for the top right-hand corner of the goal and MISSED!

The ball went miles over the bar. All the John Abbott fans were shouting and cheering and thumping each other.

They went back on to the attack. Gowland got away on the edge of our area, and Terence came out and made a point-blank save at his feet. Terence cleared the ball to Harpur and Harpur played it short to Eddie Boomer. Baldie lunged at it as Eddie turned, and Eddie's knee caught him right on the leg. Baldie gave a howl and went over.

The ball went to Dribbler, who switched it outside his man and went for the line. He pulled the ball back but it spun in the air, and what started as a centre ended up heading for the net. The goalie was going the wrong way, but he twisted round and managed to get his fist to the ball. The ball cannoned against the post and bounced down in front of me and I came sliding in and turned it into the net!

GOAL!

A Great Golden Goal for Ace Striker N. McCann had turned the tide and we were 2–1 up and on our way to win the game!

It wasn't much of a goal really, but I was back on the score sheet again after missing penalties and sitters and all sorts of soft shots, and that was all that mattered!

2–1 to Red Row Stars from a Napper McCann Golden Goal!

Before they kicked off again, Baldie was substituted. He'd been trying to bust Eddie with his tackle, so nobody was sorry he got hurt. Baldie had been going for Eddie from the kick-off, but the good thing was that Eddie *hadn't* gone for him. Eddie had thumped back and run round the place, drawing Baldie out of position and wrecking their defence.

I switched with Boom-Boom and went to centre-

forward. It confused them and in the end Jensen
came back to mark me. That pleased us because
Jensen was a brilliant player going forward, but
not so hot when he had to defend. Harpur started
throwing balls forward for me to move on to, and
Dribbler and Daniel were making runs as well.

'Come on, you Abbotts!' Jensen howled.

Gowland got away and missed a good chance.

Terence saved a good header from Roper, down
by the post, and Daniel got clear at the other end
and shot into the side netting. Then I got the ball
on the left and I turned Jensen inside out and
slipped the ball inside to Daniel and WHAM!

3–1 to Red Row Stars!

That was the way it finished.

Jensen came up beside me when we were leaving
the pitch.

'Well played,' he said, and he shook my hand.

'Hard luck,' I said. 'You gave us a good game.'

'We didn't want to lose it, no way!' he said.
Then he added, 'That guy Boomer, the one we
heard all the talk about. He's not much, is he?'

'He's okay,' I said.

'Never does anything on the ground,' Jensen
said. 'It's all up there, with the head. We reckon
we should have switched old Baldie on to you or
the winger.'

I didn't say a thing.

They may have *reckoned* it, but they hadn't *done*
it. Their toughest-tackling defender, before he had

to go off, had spent the whole match chasing round after Eddie Boomer, and we had made full use of the gaps he left when Eddie wandered.

'I wasn't offside *once*!' Eddie said, looking pleased. He knew he'd had a good game, even if he hadn't scored, and moving deep to draw Baldie out of the middle had helped to keep him onside as well.

'You owe us that one!' Bob Bridges said when I told him the result. 'That was our secret info, that was!'

'A really fine display, boys!' Mr Hope said when we were in the car. 'I know one or two other people who won't be exactly sorry you beat that lot, either!' He didn't explain what he meant, but we thought he was talking about the other teams John Abbott had kicked out of it!

'Glad to see you've got your goal touch back, Napper,' he said. 'More of the same against the Stringy Pants, eh?'

I've never heard Mr Hope call St Gabriel's the Stringy Pants before. He must have heard us saying it.

One match to go and we were in with a chance of winning the League championship!

PRIMARY SCHOOLS LEAGUE

FOURTH-ROUND RESULTS:
John Abbott 1   Red Row 3
Mill Lane 1   St Gabriel's 5
Langland 2   Monk Noxon 4

JOHN ABBOTT V. RED ROW

The surprise team of the tournament, Red Row, took the game to their opponents and did not wilt in the face of some very firm challenges indeed! C. Small, in defence, was outstanding for the winners, and Jensen and goalie Peters played well for a disappointing John Abbott team, whose chance of the title has now slipped away. Scorers: C. Small, McCann and Rooney for Red Row; Gowland for John Abbott.

MILL LANE V. ST GABRIEL'S

Mill Lane, although back to almost full strength, were no match for a confident St Gabriel's team, for whom Collins and Fish were outstanding. Goalkeeper Cleland saved a first-half penalty taken by Mill Lane's Beattie. Scorers: Bridges (2), Cleland (2) and Fish for the winners; McGaw for Mill Lane.

LANGLAND V. MONK NOXON

Langland did extremely well against a Monk Noxon team (minus schemer Ryan) who seemed to have little enthusiasm for the game. Langland went in front early on, but Peirce (3) and Holmes soon put Monk Noxon in an unassailable position. Langland's best performance of the season! Their goalscorers were Hunter and Flaydon.

LEAGUE TABLE

	P	W	D	L	F	A	Pts
St Gabriel's	4	2	2	0	23	7	6
Red Row	4	3	0	1	13	9	6
Monk Noxon	4	2	1	1	14	8	5
John Abbott	4	2	1	1	11	10	5
Mill Lane	4	1	0	3	11	12	2
Langland	4	0	0	4	3	29	0

Fifth-round fixtures:
St Gabriel's v. Red Row
Langland v. John Abbott
Monk Noxon v. Mill Lane

The League title will now be decided by the clash between Red Row, who have gone from strength to strength following a heavy defeat by Monk Noxon in the opening round, and the high-scoring, undefeated St Gabriel's side, everyone's choice as title favourites. Given their vastly superior goal difference, St Gabriel's have only to draw to clinch the title, but Red Row showed last week that they are not impressed by reputations. Should be a snorter!

John Abbott have surely lost their chance now and, with centre-half Eglet missing through injury, can hardly expect to score the sixteen goals they need to take advantage of any possible slip by St Gabriel's. Langland, who improved vastly last week, will be in no mood to give goals away to any challenger.

Monk Noxon entertain Mill Lane and should win, given the disappointing form of their visitors.

D. W. Overend (Secretary)

8. Who Plays in the Big Match?

We were out behind the school on Wednesday, practising set-pieces with the bike shed as our goal, when Joe Fish and Knocker Lewis came through the fence, looking important.

'Spies!' Cyril shouted. 'Beware spies!'

'Shut your mouth, Cyril,' Knocker said.

'Oh yes?' said Cyril. 'Who's going to shut it for me?' Cyril said it, but he didn't sound very fierce. We all know what Knocker is like.

'*You* shut up, Knocker,' said Joe. Then he said, 'Did you lot hear about our big match?'

'What about the match?' I said. I was afraid it might have been put off.

'It's been switched to Owen Lane, where County play!' Joe announced.

Everybody started cheering and shouting. County are a real team in the Northern Combination, and Owen Lane is their ground. It is a proper ground, with floodlights and dressing-rooms and a grandstand.

'What about floodlights?' said Cyril. 'We ought to play under floodlights!'

'Mr Overend used to play for County after he left Barnsley,' said Joe. We didn't know that Mr Overend had played for Barnsley, but it didn't matter. 'He had a talk with Mr Trotman, the County Manager, and they've switched the game to Saturday afternoon at Owen Lane because it's the League championship decider!'

'Like City against United!' shouted Cyril.

'Liverpool against Everton!' I said.

We all thought it was great that we would be playing on a proper pitch, and everybody got excited.

'You're all like little kids!' Avril said when she heard us talking. 'It's only a little kids' football match!'

'It's not!' said Helena Bellow. 'It's the Championship decider! It's the biggest match this school has ever been in, and I think we should all be supporters now, so there!'

'We're supposed to be an Anti-Football-Team Club,' said Avril. 'We don't support them.'

Helena said they should have a vote on it, and Helena won!

'You needn't think *I'm* going to support you,' Avril said afterwards.

'Nobody wants you to!' Cyril told her, but afterwards Ugly Irma Bankworth came up and told Terence that the Anti-Football-Team Club would all be supporting Red Row Stars in the big match.

'Miss Fellows says we have to, so we are,' said Ugly Irma.

'Most of us would have been, anyway,' said Helena.

That was our support fixed up, but it wasn't that that was worrying us. It was our team.

We had to leave somebody out.

Marky Bellow and Scottie Watts were both back at school and they wanted to be in the team, but so did Scuddy Rodgers and Joe Small, and they had played in the match against John Abbott, which put us through to the decider.

'We've got to drop *somebody*,' said Terence.

'Bet it'll be me,' said Peter Scott.

He was right, but it wasn't a matter of dropping him. Nobody except him had ever thought he would be in the match, because he was only the sub against John Abbott, when we were short of two of our regular players.

'It's up to the Selection Committee to pick the team, Pete,' said Harpur. 'You'll have the same chance as anybody else.'

'I'll bet,' said Peter.

We were sorry for him, but it was his own fault. Peter had had stacks and stacks of chances to play in the team because he is big, but he never did anything except stand around complaining about not getting the ball.

We held a special meeting of the Selection Committee to pick the big-match team. It was held in the bike shed on Thursday after training, and Terence was Chairman because he is our Player-Manager.

Terence had a good idea. He said that instead of starting to argue about who *wasn't* in the team, we should start off by picking the people who *had* to be in it, and then it would be easier to decide between the rest.

'Start with us,' said Cyril, and he wrote down our names. Then we added Harry Haxwell and John Deacon and Daniel Rooney, even though Daniel hadn't been playing well.

'Eddie Boomer,' said Cyril.

'Boom-Boom was a waste of time against John Abbott and not much better against Mill Lane,' Harpur said. 'He keeps getting offside and he doesn't pass the ball. Anyway, he's a striker, and Napper is our striker. Napper's much better than he is. When did Eddie ever pass to anybody?'

It was about three times, as far as I could remember.

'You don't want him to be in the team because you don't *like* him,' said Cyril. 'I vote Eddie has to be in the team.'

Harpur frowned. He was fed up with Eddie, because all the little kids had been going round for weeks saying Eddie was our best-ever five-goal centre-forward because he'd got five goals. Harpur is a very good footballer, the sort who thinks about what he is doing. Harpur can spot what ought to be done and then do it!

'He's not your sort of player, Harpur,' I said.

'But we do need him in the team. He makes room for the rest of us to play.'

'He's not good enough,' said Harpur. 'We know Knocker and Joe and Pete Cross and Gary Watson aren't stupid. They won't let him draw them out of position like John Abbott did. We have to *play* to beat the Stringy Pants . . . and Boom-Boom doesn't know how to. He keeps on running, but he's slow and bad on the ground, and he can't beat a man except by knocking him down. He keeps getting offside as well.'

'He's good in the air,' I said.

'So?'

'Joe Fish usually beats me in the air. I can beat him on the ground. If we use Boom-Boom for high balls, knocking them down for me, or heading in goals himself, we can play twin strikers!'

'Tweedledum and Tweedledee!' said Cyril. 'Guess who is Tweedle-D U M B!'

We took a vote. It was three to one against Harpur.

'We know he's not your sort of player,' said Terence to Harpur. 'But we can still use him in the team. We need strength as well as skill.'

'Probably get sent off for fouling,' Harpur said.

'If Baldie doesn't get sent off, I don't see why Eddie should,' Terence said. The refs and the teachers had all made a lot of fuss about rough play, but the only player who'd been sent off was Marky, and that was for calling H. Death names.

'Football *is* rough, anyway,' said Cyril.

We reckoned that most of Eddie's fouls happened because he was bigger than his opponents, and they bounced off when he hit them. Maybe some of the refs thought Baldie was the same, but he wasn't.

Dribbler Wilson's was the last name we added to the list. We thought he might be too small to manage the big pitch at Owen Lane, but he was brilliant too, and we thought he would turn Knocker Lewis inside out! The last time we played the Stringy Pants, Knocker got sent off for kicking Dribbler deliberately after Dribbler had made him look silly. St Gabriel's had to play with ten men, which served Knocker right.

This was the list of 'must-be-in-the-team' players:

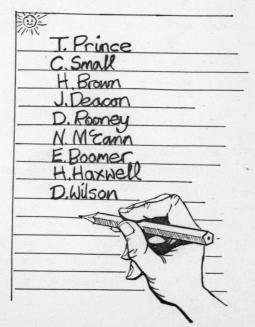

T. Prince
C. Small
H. Brown
J. Deacon
D. Rooney
N. McCann
E. Boomer
H. Haxwell
D. Wilson

We looked at the list, and then we added three names – two players and a sub – to make up the team that would take the field on Red Row Stars' greatest-ever challenge!

9. Red Row Stars v. St Gabriel's

PRIMARY SCHOOLS LEAGUE
FIFTH ROUND
Red Row P.S. v. St Gabriel's P.S.
Referee: B. Simpson
Linesmen: H. Death (red flag)
D. W. Overend (yellow flag)
Venue: Owen Lane Stadium, Warne

We drove down to Owen Lane Stadium, and when we went into the dressing-room we found all our kit laid out on the benches round the room, with shirts and socks and shorts for each player, and fresh laces for tie-ups. On the noticeboard was a copy of the match programme, which D. W. Overend had run off on his school's copying machine.

It was great. Mr Hope brought us down half an hour before the game and we had a walk out on the pitch. Then we came in and got changed, and he said he wasn't going to tell us anything because we had been through it all before and now there was only one thing to do . . . go out and play.

This is the team I led out of the tunnel on to the pitch at Owen Lane Stadium for the Most Important Match in the History of Our School!

T. Prince

M. Bellow   S. Rodgers

C. Small

J. Deacon   H. Haxwell

N. McCann (Capt.)   H. Brown

D. Rooney   E. Boomer   D. Wilson

Substitute S. Watts

Trainer Mr Hope

Travelling Official Miss E. Fellows

We brought Marky in and moved Scuddy across to replace Joe Small. That meant we had to leave Scottie out of the team, which was hard luck on Scottie. He took it well. He went up to Scuddy and said, 'Best of luck, Scuddy!' and we all felt sorry for him, because it was the first-ever match that Scottie had missed when he was fit to play.

'You might get on in the second half,' I told him.

'It's not the same as being in the team, is it?' Scottie said.

He joined P. Scott and Duncan and Joe and

Jonathan Ramsey and Douglas King, who were all sitting beside Mr Hope on the team bench as I went up to shake hands with Joe Fish and toss up.

I lost the toss, and St Gabriel's decided to play down towards the scoreboard end. We lined up to kick off, and suddenly the pitch and the grandstand and the floodlights and everything looked ginormous. Then the ref, B. Simpson, blew his whistle, and we kicked off and I had to forget about everything except playing.

We went straight on to the attack. We had decided that I would play up alongside Eddie to begin with, hoping that Joe Fish wouldn't know which one of us he was supposed to mark, but it didn't take Joe long to sort it out. He went to mark me, and they moved Knocker Lewis into the middle to take out Eddie.

'This ought to be good!' Joe said to me when Knocker and Eddie were picking themselves up from the ground after their first tussle. Neither of them could play football much, but they were both going at it hammer and tongs.

The best thing about the opening minutes was the way Daniel Rooney got into the game. He was taking on his man down the right wing, and twice he went past him and slung centres across the St Gabriel's goal. On the first one, Hugh Cleland came off his line and clawed the ball out of the air for a good save. I almost got on the end of the second, but Joe managed to flick the ball off my foot, putting it behind for a corner.

Daniel went across to take the corner. I thought I would go short, so I ran out to him and he tapped the ball to me, and Pete Carnforth came running across to cut me out. Joe Fish had shouted to Pete to do it because he was afraid of getting drawn from the centre. Pete held off, but I managed to get an angle and slung my centre across. Harpur was going for it and Joe Fish brought him down.

The ref's whistle blew?

PENALTY!

Joe Fish stood staring at the ref as though he couldn't believe it. Then he put his hands on his head and walked away.

Eddie Boomer ran across and got the ball. He put it on the spot.

Everybody looked at me.

Everybody was remembering what I'd done against John Abbott, blasting the ball over the bar. I suppose they all thought I would call up Harpur, who is a dead-ball expert, or Harry, but I didn't.

I was going to take it myself. I was going to take it because if I didn't take it, then I couldn't say I was a Demon Goalscorer any more. Goalscorers have to score goals, and that means risking missing chances too!

I put the ball on the spot.

I walked back.

The ref blew his whistle.
I ran up.
WHAM!
Goal!

1–0 to Red Row Stars!
I'd scored!
All our team came charging up, and I went down
under them. We were 1–0 up and winning the
League championship decider and we were going
to be the champions of the Primary Schools League
at our very first attempt through a great victory in
our very first game in a proper football stadium.
'Come on! Let's get into it!' Joe Fish shouted.
Our fans were shouting and dancing about when
they kicked off, and straight away the ball went out

to Neil Collins on the wing. Neil took it and hood-winked Harry Haxwell, then he turned inside and beat Scuddy for speed. He got to the edge of our area and unleashed a superdrive.

Terence took off! He went up in the air and arched back and just managed to tip the ball up and over the bar!

Everybody shouted and cheered and clapped Terence for making a brilliant save just when an equalizer would have put St Gabriel's back in the game.

Joe Fish came up for the corner, and I went to go with him, but then I saw Eddie was going in-stead, so I hung back and found Knocker Lewis breathing down my neck.

'What's wrong, Knocker?' I said. 'Looking for someone?'

'Ha ha!' Knocker said. He'd come really tight against me, which I thought was great because I knew if I could get the ball I could do him for speed.

Neil Collins took the corner and Bob Bridges got in and volleyed the ball from the edge of the area, but Terence caught it without even moving and, almost in the same moment, he slung the ball wide to Harpur, who had come deep to get it.

Harpur took one look at the set-up and fired the ball deep into the St Gabriel's half for me to sprint on to.

Harpur pumped the ball far down the wing,

and by the time Knocker had turned round I was on my way. I got the ball just outside the area, saw Hugh Cleland come rushing out and drilled the ball past him, hard and low into the corner of the net!

2–0 to Red Row Stars, and the game had only just started!

Here's how we did it:

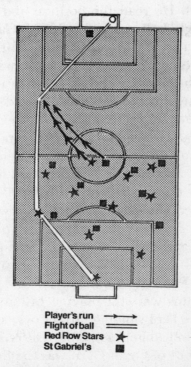

Player's run	→———→
Flight of ball	═══════
Red Row Stars	★
St Gabriel's	■

The great thing about the goal was its simplicity. Mr Hope had told us to look out for big gaps because we would be playing on a much larger pitch than we are used to. Owen Lane is almost Wembley size, and it certainly felt like it! Knocker had insisted on coming up to crowd me, and their team had all gone forward for the corner. There were other good things about the goal. Terence's throw was quick and accurate. Harpur had taken up position well. Harpur didn't mess about when he got the ball. He read the position and played his long through ball perfectly. N. McCann's finish was BRILLIANT! The other thing that pleased us was that we had *planned* it. Not the way we plan set-pieces, because we didn't know exactly how it would occur, but the *idea* was planned.

Another GOLDEN GOAL for N. McCann!

'You should have cut him out, Knocker,' said Joe Fish, but the next time they got a corner he stayed back and did the covering, and let Knocker go up into our area. The ball came across and Eddie floored Knocker. We thought it was going to be a penalty, but the referee waved play on. He was a good ref, B. Simpson. He had a proper ref's kit and an F. A. badge. So had the linesmen. It was like a Cup Final at Wembley!

Neil Collins was still playing brilliantly on the wing and he kept slinging crosses over the area for Gerry Cleland to get on to, but Gerry was getting no change out of Cyril. Cyril was the first to every tackle and he was beating Gerry to the ball in the air. It looked as if we were coasting to victory, because every time we went on the attack Dribbler was getting past his man and Daniel was beating his and I already had two goals and Boom-Boom was keeping Knocker Lewis tied up.

Then they got away down the wing. Bob Bridges went wide, and he fired a long ball into the area.

'Mine!' Terence shouted, and he came out to take it at the high point and . . .

Missed!

Gerry Cleland took the ball on the bounce, and nodded it into the back of our net! He went down on his knees with his fists clenched, and yelled at the crowd behind the goal. The crowd behind the goal was John Deacon's mother, Helena Bellow, and Mrs Cleland. They had come in late and were heading for the grandstand. Mrs Deacon didn't look very pleased at being yelled at.

Terence fished the ball out of the net and drop-kicked it back to the centre. Then he stood with his hands on his hips, looking really disgusted with himself.

Terence's mistake seemed to put everybody off. For the first time in the game, Bob Bridges got past John Deacon and Marky, and twice he got over centres. Terence stayed glued to his line both times. The first time, Harry Haxwell had to dive in and head over our bar. It was so close that we all thought it was going in. The second time, Knocker Lewis got on the end of it after Scuddy had missed his clearance, and Knocker blazed the ball over the bar.

'Your man, Eddie!' Harpur called.

Eddie looked at me.

'I thought I was supposed to stay upfield,' he said.

We were starting to argue all over again. Mr Hope came off the bench to shout at us, but Miss Fellows pulled his coat and he sat down again.

He should have shouted harder.

Joe Fish played a long ball down the middle and Sam Welby headed it sideways and Bob Bridges took it on the volley and smacked it right through Terence's arms into the back of our net.

2–2!

2–2 when we had been 2–0 up and heading for an easy win.

'Why didn't you save it?' Harry shouted at Terence.

Terence shrugged.

It was a shot he would have saved easily in most games, even though Bob hit it hard. It was hit straight at Terence.

'Don't know how you missed it!' Harry said. 'What a goalie!'

They went on the attack again. Knocker fired in a deep cross and Terence came out and fumbled the ball. He dropped it, and Harry slid in to clear for a corner.

'Wake up, Terence!' Harpur shouted.

The corner came across and Terence started out of his goal, then stopped, and was beaten by Joe Fish's header, which hit the underside of the bar and bounced down in front of Cyril. Cyril took a huge swing at the ball and mis-hit it, because he was falling into the goal as he swung. He banged the ball, and it came out and cannoned into John Deacon's face and back towards our goal. Terence and Knocker Lewis and Boom-Boom all went for the ball at the same time and Knocker got it, but Terence stuck out his arm and the ball spun off him and went round the post.

Corner kick.

They didn't get a chance to take it because the whistle went for half-time.

Half-time. It was amazing! The match had gone so fast that I didn't think it could *possibly* be half-time. We came dragging off the pitch, thinking about the way we'd let the Stringy Pants back into the game after being 2–0 up.

Terence was the last man off the pitch and into the tunnel. His face was bright red.

'Cheer up, Terence,' Mr Hope said when he saw him.

There were drinks for us in the dressing-room, and Mr Hope didn't shout at us or anything. He said he thought we could still win it if we tightened up at the back, cut out the mistakes, didn't panic and remembered about the wide-open spaces.

'Especially the wide-open spaces!' he said. 'This team isn't much at the back. Rooney, McCann, little Dribbler there, you've got the beating of them.

I want to see the ball played into the gaps behind them . . . big gaps, bit pitch, remember. You're faster than they are. Take them on the turn and you can beat them.'

Terence was the last man down the tunnel at the beginning of the second half.

'He's gone all jammy-fingered,' Harry said to me.

'We wouldn't be here if it wasn't for Terence,' I said.

It was St Gabriel's turn to kick off, and they were attacking the dressing-room end. They went back on to the attack and straight away Terence fumbled another ball right on the edge of his area. In the end he had to tackle Roy Prescot with his feet and play the ball away for a throw-in.

'Augh, Roy!' Bob Bridges shouted. Bob had been in the centre unmarked, and he would have scored if Roy had managed to take advantage of Terence's fumble and get the ball across.

I started to drift back because they were getting on top of us.

'Stay where you are, Napper!' Harpur shouted, but where I was I wasn't getting the ball.

One of the reasons that I wasn't getting the ball was John Deacon. He had got a bad bang in the face in the first half, when he ran into Cyril's goal-line clearance and almost headed it back into our net. The ball had hit him in the mouth, and John's nose started to bleed. Mr Hope fixed it at half-time, but it had begun to bleed again, and he didn't look too well.

'You all right, John?' I asked him.

He nodded, but the next time the ball came up he came across to me and he said, 'No, I'm not. I'm going off!'

John went off!

Scottie was up off the bench in no time, taking off his tracksuit and bouncing up and down. Miss Fellows had given him some chewing-gum and he came on chewing like mad and ran across to take John's place, absolutely determined to show us all that he should never have been dropped.

Neil Collins got the ball and took Scotty on.

Crunch! Scottie came away with it and flighted a good ball forward. Eddie got up above Joe Fish and headed the ball down to me and I tried a first-timer, but Hugh Cleland saved it easily.

Then Scottie got tangled up with Pete Crowshaw and won the ball. Pete should have been marking Daniel, but he had come forward. Scottie played an intelligent ball down the wing to Daniel and Daniel took it, controlled it, beat off another challenge and cut the ball back from the goal-line on to Eddie's head. Eddie got up above everybody and headed down, and Knocker Lewis managed to put it behind the goal for a corner.

I went to take it.

Harpur had moved up, and Eddie had moved to the back of the box, taking Joe Fish with him.

Knocker was on the post. Cyril was waiting on the edge of the area. I could play it deep to Eddie, or short to Harpur, or I could swing it wide and hope that Cyril would come in and meet it around the penalty spot.

'Napper!' Harry shouted.

He had come belting up, short. I played the ball back to him.

One of the St Gabriel's backs came pounding across and at the same time Joe Fish started to scream 'OUT!' at them, so we would be offside. Harry controlled the ball, feinted to go inside and slipped the ball back to me.

Knocker Lewis was still on the goalpost. We had beaten their offside trap and I was right through, with only Knocker and the goalie to beat, but I was on the goal-line at an impossible angle.

Knocker came out of the goal and headed for me, but over his shoulder I spotted what I was looking for. St Gabriel's were totally wrong-footed, and a familiar jet-propelled windmill was heading for the goal.

I curled the ball across, well over Hugh Cleland's head, and all Boom-Boom had to do was to nod it into the net!

GOAL!

3–2 to Red Row!

'Okay! Okay! We're NOT finished,' Joe Fish shouted, and St Gabriel's got the ball and kicked off and went straight on to the attack.

Cyril hooked one off the line.

Scuddy only just got in a tackle on Bob Bridges which stopped him scoring.

Terence saved a drive from Gerry Cleland with his knee.

Then Harry Haxwell got the ball from a throw-in and played it deep again. I managed to get on to it, and Hugh Cleland came belting out of goal.

I lobbed him.

GOAL!

Another Napper McCann Super Golden Goal, giving me a hat-trick in my first-ever game in a proper stadium, which was also the League championship decider!

4–2 against St Gabriel's, and up till then they had only let in seven goals in four games, which made us look really good. I think the difference was that they played better on small pitches. The big pitch at Owen Lane was definitely an advantage to us.

Joe and Knocker and everybody went on the attack, and then Terence started saving again.

He took off and turned a shot from Gerry Cleland round the post. Next he held a drive from Bob Bridges and another one from Neil Collins when Neil should have scored. Neil was clean through after a neat pass from Joe Fish, but he hit the ball straight at Terence and Terence held it.

'Come on, Red Row!' Miss Fellows shouted.

All our reserves were up from the bench shouting and cheering, and our fans were on their feet too in the grandstand, and suddenly I looked at the clock at the end of the ground and I knew what all the fuss was about.

Full-time!

4–2 to Red Row!

We had won the championship of the Primary Schools League and the Dr Murray Cup which went with it on our first-ever season in the competition, and there was no way anyone could argue about it because we were the better team on the day, and that was it!

'Well done, Napper,' Joe Fish said, coming up to me. 'Reckon the big pitch did for us!'

All our supporters were cheering and clapping, and we had to go up and get the Dr Murray Cup and our medals. Dr Murray shook us by the hand and Mrs Murray was there with her two daughters and her titchy son, but Mrs Murray wasn't pleased when Eddie Boomer stood on her foot.

The other really exciting thing that happened to me was when D. W. Overend, who used to play for Barnsley, came into our dressing-room after the game. He is the League Secretary as well as being championship-decider linesman, and he said to Mr Hope, 'Well, Bruce, great game! You've got some fine players here!' Then he spotted me and said, 'You're the kid who got the hat-trick, aren't you? Will you still be at Red Row next year?'

I said I would.

'You'll be knocking on the door of the Inter-League team then,' he said. 'Nice to see how you would fit in with young Ryan alongside you!'

INTER-LEAGUE!

'That rather depends on whether we can scrape together enough players to make up a Red Row team,' said Mr Hope.

'Course we will, Sir!' shouted Cyril, jumping around with his medal in his hand.

'*You* won't be in it, Cyril,' Mr Hope pointed out. 'You'll have gone on to scale greater heights, your career in secondary education!'

'Doesn't matter!' said Cyril. 'RED ROW FOR EVER!'

We all started shouting it too. It wasn't true, but we all wished it was.

Our team was the Greatest Ever in the History of Red Row School. We had won the championship of the Primary Schools League at our first attempt. We had a cup and medals and we had played a BRILLIANT game in the decider on a proper football ground with grandstands and we reckoned that was G-R-E-A-T!

Here we are with our medals. The one holding the cup is Douglas King, and the one with the lid

on his head is Cyril. Dribbler Wilson is the one on Eddie Boomer's shoulders, and Terence is the one being kissed by Helena Bellow. Terence says it was *awful*. Ugly Irma is the one who has just tripped over the bucket, and our Avril is the one she is sitting on.

I'm the one with the ball. Mr Hope and Mr Thompson, who is the Headmaster of St Gabriel's, presented it to me because I got a hat-trick. I felt like a real SUPER STAR!

PRIMARY SCHOOLS LEAGUE
Bulletin No. 6

FIFTH-ROUND RESULTS:

St Gabriel's 2   Red Row 4
Langland 0   John Abbott 9
Monk Noxon 3   Mill Lane 1

ST GABRIEL'S V. RED ROW

This game was played at Owen Lane Stadium, Warne, a fitting setting for a League championship decider! The two extremely young teams did not allow themselves to be overawed by their setting, although the 'wide-open spaces' of the ground played their part in the end result. St Gabriel's, attacking freely as they have done all season, were deservedly beaten by a Red Row team which, while often under pressure, made full use of the long ball. Rooney, McCann, Brown and Small were outstanding for the winners, while Fish, Lewis and Collins did well for St Gabriel's, for whom Bridges and Cleland scored. McCann (3) and Boomer scored for Red Row. Fortunately, Dr Murray was able to attend the game and present the cup he has so kindly donated to the League, and the Committee would like to convey their thanks to him and also to the stadium authorities for their cooperation in making the League's 'show-piece game' such a great success.

LANGLAND V. JOHN ABBOTT

John Abbott, as expected, ran out easy winners of a game which never rose to any heights, so great was the disparity in size between the two teams. Gowland (4), Priest (2), Dubray (2) and Jensen scored for the winners.

MONK NOXON V. MILL LANE

This typical end-of-season game lacked bite, but Monk Noxon played well enough to suggest that, but for some unfortunate injuries, they might have been worthy of better things. No doubt they will rise again, like the Phoenix! Walls (2) and Ryan scored for Monk Noxon; Russell replied for Mill Lane. Following the game, Mill Lane were presented with the Sherrard Cup, awarded on the basis of fair-play points collected through the period of the competition. Well done, Mill Lane!

LEAGUE TABLE

	P	W	D	L	F	A	Pts
Red Row	5	4	0	1	17	11	8
John Abbott	5	3	1	1	20	10	7
Monk Noxon	5	3	1	1	17	9	7
St Gabriel's	5	2	2	1	25	11	6
Mill Lane	5	1	0	4	12	15	2
Langland	5	0	0	5	3	38	0

League winners (Dr Murray Cup): Red Row P.S.
Runners-up: John Abbott P.S.
Fair play (Sherrard Cup): Mill Lane P.S.
D. W. Overend (Secretary)

Red Row Stars:
Summary of Appearances and Goalscorers

v. *Monk Noxon* (Home)
Team: T. Prince   M. Bellow   H. Haxwell
E. Boomer   S. Watts   J. Deacon   H. Brown
D. Rooney   N. McCann   P. Scott   D. Wilson
Sub: D. Forbes
Result: 0–5

v. *Langland* (Away)
Team: T. Prince   J. Deacon   H. Haxwell
C. Small   S. Watts   J. Small   P. Scott
H. Brown   D. Rooney   E. Boomer   D. Wilson
Sub: S. Rodgers
Result: 7–1   Goalscorers: Boomer (5), C. Small, Wilson

v. *Mill Lane* (Home)
Team: T. Prince   S. Rodgers   J. Deacon
C. Small   J. Small   D. Rooney   P. Scott
N. McCann   J. Ramsey   E. Boomer   D. King
Sub: —
Result: 3–2   Goalscorers: Boomer (2), King

v. *John Abbott* (Away)
Team: T. Prince   S. Rodgers   J. Small
J. Deacon   C. Small   H. Haxwell   D. Rooney
N. McCann   E. Boomer   H. Brown   D. Wilson
Sub: P. Scott
Result: 3–1   Goalscorers: C. Small, Rooney, McCann

v. *St Gabriel's* (Neutral Ground)
Team: T. Prince   M. Bellow   S. Rodgers
J. Deacon   C. Small   H. Haxwell   D. Rooney
N. McCann   E. Boomer   H. Brown   D. Wilson
Sub: S. Watts
Result: 4–2   Goalscorers: McCann (3), Boomer

Football Notes
by Ms E. Fellows

The School Team played magnificently this year, carrying off the championship of the Primary Schools League and the coveted Dr Murray Cup which goes with it. Our congratulations to all concerned.

The following players took part:

Prince, Terence Another fine season for Terence, although a burst of nerves in the final match almost proved fatal. Terence is improving his game steadily, and his good judgement and quick reactions stand him in good stead. A fine player.

Bellow, Mark Mark has done well again this term, firmly establishing himself in the first-team squad. Strong and combative.

Haxwell, Harold Harry has played his part in the season's triumph, and is exercising much greater control of himself, both on and off the field. A tenacious tackler.

Deacon, John A steady midfield player, whose influence has been felt throughout the team.

Watts, Andrew A never-say-die defender, Andrew perhaps lacks concentration, but he is a willing worker who makes up in energy what he lacks in skill.

Scott, Peter Peter has had another disappointing season. He will not improve until he learns to get more involved in the game.

Brown, Harpur Our 'star schemer' excelled himself this term, and can look forward to his footballing future with confidence. A fine all-rounder with the ability to tackle hard and distribute the ball.

Rooney, Daniel Daniel has failed to make much impact this season, but stood up well in our testing League decider, where he more than took the measure of the opposing full-back.

McCann, Bernard Bernard (Napper!), usually a striker, tried other roles this term, but his hat-trick in the last game confirmed that leading the attack is his natural role. Captain of the team and an excellent player, he is lacking only in inches!

Small, Joseph Continues to improve, and has taken his chances well in the team.

Forbes, Duncan Limited to one appearance this term due to pressing musical commitments, Duncan is a promising player for the future.

Wilson, Donald 'Dribbler' has not made his usual contribution in matches this term. A useful player, who tends to fade out of the game for long intervals.

Small, Cyril The rock on which our defence is built! Coming back after a serious injury, Cyril proved diffident in the opening matches, but has now regained his usual crunching form in the middle of the field!

Ramsey, Jonathan Played only one game, and tried hard.

Boomer, Edward A clumsy player, who has done his best to fit into a dual striking role with McCann. He is honest and energetic, but deficient in the basic skills, although his heading ability is a marked advantage.

King, Douglas Called up in an emergency, Douglas played with great spirit and notched a goal which proved vital to our League campaign. He and Ramsey will no doubt be the 'Stars' of tomorrow!

Our thanks are due once again to Mr Hogan, the caretaker, for opening the hall on match days, and also to the many spectators who turned up to cheer the team, particularly in our big match at the Owen Lane Stadium.

Well done, everybody!

Ms E. Fellows

Also by Martin Waddell

NAPPER GOES FOR GOAL

It was Napper McCann who first had the idea of forming the school football team. He was fed up with being called names by the boys from St Gabriel's Primary just because his own school, Red Row Primary, was small and didn't have a team. So he called a meeting and thus began the glorious history of the Red Row Stars. But it wasn't all glorious, by any means!

NAPPER STRIKES AGAIN

Now in their second season, Napper and the Red Row Stars are convinced they can win the Spring Cup – but they meet so many problems, they begin to wonder if they'll ever get through in one piece. Lots of fun, excitement and useful tips for young football fans.

TALES FROM THE SHOP THAT NEVER SHUTS
Martin Waddell

In these five highly entertaining stories the Gang dig for Viking treasure, are frightened that a sea monster has eaten Biddy, discover that McGlone needs glasses, look after the Shop That Never Shuts on their own, and give Biddy a birthday party. Told with immense humour, the adventures of these delightful characters will charm all who read them.

THE FOX OF SKELLAND
Rachel Dixon

Samantha's never liked the old custom of Foxing Day – the fox costume especially gives her the creeps. So when Jason and Rib, children of the new publicans at The Fox and Lady, find the costume and Jason wears it to the fancy-dress disco, she's sure something awful will happen.

Then Sam's old friend Joseph sees the ghost of the Lady and her fox. Has she really come back to exact vengeance on the village? Or has her appearance got something to do with the spate of burglaries in the area?

WOLF

Gillian Cross

Cassy has never understood the connection between the secret midnight visitor to her nan's flat and her sudden trips to stay with her mother. But this time it seems different. She finds her mother living in a squat with her boyfriend Lyall and his son Robert. Lyall has devised a theatrical event for children on wolves, and Cassy is soon deeply involved in presenting it. Perhaps too involved – for she begins to sense a very real and terrifying wolf stalking her.

THE OUTSIDE CHILD

Nina Bawden

Imagine suddenly discovering you have a step-brother and -sister no one has ever told you about! It's the most exciting thing that's ever happened to Jane, and she can't wait to meet them. Perhaps at last she will become part of a 'proper' family, instead of for ever being the outside child. So begins a long search for her brother and sister, but when she finally does track them down, Jane finds there are still more surprises in store!

HANDS UP! AT JUG VALLEY JUNIORS

Anne Digby

Ben couldn't guess the trouble he would cause when he accidentally kicks Charlie Smith's old football into the rector's garden. When Ben and his friends in Handles & Spouts search the garden after school, there's no sign of the ball. They get Charlie a new one, but Charlie is desperate to find the old ball. Who can have taken it, and why does Charlie want it back so badly? Handles & Spouts have some surprises in store in this third story of a fantastic new series.

THE PHOTOFIT MYSTERY AT JUG VALLEY JUNIORS

Anne Digby

Esme asks the members of Handles & Spouts to watch the house she and her father used to live in. It's supposed to be empty since her father moved to New Zealand to get a better job, and she moved in with her aunt. Missing her father terribly, Esme has noticed little things which have been moved, as though someone is still living in the old house.

Handles & Spouts decide to piece together a photo-fit description to identify the mysterious person in the fourth brilliant adventure of this exciting series.

MISSING

James Duffy

One evening, Kate Prescott is approached by a man in a large black car. He seems friendly and says he knows her mother, so Kate accepts a lift from him. It doesn't take Kate long, however, to realize the dreadful mistake she has made. But will the chief of police be convinced that she really is in danger when she's reported missing?

MIGHTIER THAN THE SWORD

Clare Bevan

Adam had always felt he was somehow special, different from the rest of the family, but could he really be a modern-day King Arthur, the legendary figure they're learning about at school? Inspired by the stories they are hearing in class, Adam and his friends become absorbed in a complex game of knights and good deeds. All they need is a worthy cause for which to fight. So when they discover that the local pond is under threat, Adam's knights are ready to join battle with the developers.

Reality and legend begin to blur in this lively, original story about an imaginative boy who doesn't let a mere wheelchair get in his way of adventure.